MW01241067

TWEAKER CREATURES

First Edition Trade Paperback

ISBN: 9798780354277

Cover, layout and interior
K. Trap Jones

www.theevilcookie.com

PROLOGUE

———

The alleyway behind the old strip mall had always been a mess, but was exceptionally filthy now that the businesses were abandoned and the apartments flanking the opposite side of said alley were just as rundown as ever. Trevor used the alley as a short cut to get home after band practice. He carried a B.C. Rich Warlock guitar in a nice solid shell case. The guitar was his pride and joy. He wouldn't let anything happen to it.

Trevor hated the alleyway behind the old Ralphs strip mall, even before everything went to shit. It smelled of piss and beer, was littered with glass and random detritus, and there always seemed to be homeless men asleep on old mattresses from the roach motel apartments or leaning against a wall sharing a crack pipe.

If it wasn't for saving a good twenty minutes walk, Trevor wouldn't step foot in this particular alley. But he figured let one of the bums fuck with him. He'd kick all their asses. Especially how he felt right about now, high off a good band practice.

"Hey!" came a voice off to his right.

Trevor knew better than to look. The Cardinal rule when dealing with tweakers or bums was to never look them in the eye. That was as good as an invitation. But, in this case, the voice was so *off*. It was kind of gritty, almost evil sounding. Kind of like the heavy metal music he played with his friends up on First Avenue. Trevor pivoted his head to the right, figuring he'd get just a glance at the guy.

"Come here." The guy crouched within a pile of discarded boxes and the remnants of a couch that had been lit on fire at some point. He was hidden in shadow, eyes blazing.

Trevor shrugged him off and kept walking. Rule number two when dealing with those types was to ignore them. Act like they weren't even there.

But that didn't always work.

The man's voice came again. "Hey, I got something for you. Don't fuckin' walk away from me like that."

Trevor turned, prepared to dismiss the man again, but the guy was right behind him, which startled Trevor, nearly causing him to drop his guitar case.

"I got something here for you," the man said. "Some good stuff. You gotta try it."

Shaking his head, Trevor said, "I don't do that shit, man."

Gritting his teeth, the man reached out and grabbed Trevor by the back of his throat. Trevor yelped and swung around. With the clunky guitar case held in one hand, he didn't have enough torque on it to give a good swing. The guitar case hit the man's legs, and he kicked it, which caused Trevor to drop it.

"Hey!" Trevor yelled, "What the fuck, man? Let go of me!"

That's when Trevor saw what he was dealing with. The man's face was twisted up in shreds of melting skin like he'd been bathing in caustic acid. He smiled like a corpse, all rotting teeth, where he still had them, and the breath emanating from that foul maw was like he ate dead rats for breakfast.

"Fuck your guitar," the man said, his filthy hand still gripped tight around Trevor's throat. With his other hand he pulled out a rather large bag of dope from the pocket of severely stained pants. "You won't need the guitar after you try this shit. You won't need anything."

Somehow the man grinned, which caused him to appear even more menacing. His eyes weren't quite centered.

"I told you," Trevor said as she squirmed to get out of the guy's grip, "I don't do that shit!"

The man's eyes deepened. "Well, you better start, you little fuck. Soon enough everybody's gonna be doing this new shit."

That's when several other tweakers came out of nowhere. Something about them was off, but Trevor didn't get a good look at them before everything went sideways.

"Leave me the fuck alone," Trevor said.

The hand squeezing Trevor's throat let go and he turned to run, but before he could take a step, a foot was trust in his way, causing him to trip and fall on his face. Hands grabbed at his legs, holding him tight, and then another set of hands wrapped around his head from above, cradling his cranium with the fingertips grazing his lower jaw. Trevor flailed, but there were too many of them. The ragged fingernails pinched the soft flesh beneath his jaw, pushing until the skin gave purchase. Trevor screamed, and that's when the tweaker gripping his head pulled. The others held tight to his legs and abdomen. Trevor's screams were loud and shrieking, more so than his vocals only a half hour ago during band practice. Vertebrae cracked, his screams hit a new level of agony as the realization sunk in that he was indeed dying, and then another sickening sound erupted as the tweaker pulling his head managed to break Trevor's spine and extract the head in a torrent of blood and dangling arteries and veins.

The captor of the head ran through the alleyway with his prize. Another pulled out the B.C. Rich guitar and started strumming the strings while the others played with the rest of the corpse.

CHAPTER 1

––

The decision to go AWOL from the police academy wasn't hard for Amber to make, not after the devastating call from her mother. It was a tear-filled conversation, on Mom's part, explaining that Amber's sister Erin had been missing for days and the El Cajon Police Department were doing little to find her, being that there was no evidence she'd been abducted and the fact crime rates skyrocketed in record time. As far as the law was concerned, teenaged girls often ran away from home, more than likely returning when they needed money or realized they made a big mistake.

"You're kidding. They're not doing anything?"

After a sob, her mother said, "They took a report, but... ah, they said this sort of thing happens all the time. Amber, I think she's been using drugs."

"What? You serious?"

"She got really skinny. And distant, kind of like..."

"Yeah, I know," Amber answered quickly. Neither she nor her mother wanted to revisit those awful years. She certainly hoped that Erin wasn't following in her footsteps.

"I looked through her room and found a little box with some things in it that I think have to do with drugs, but I... I don't know anything about this stuff. I never did any of that drug stuff. I tried raising you girls the best I could, what with working and... your father not around."

Amber closed her eyes tight, fighting back tears.

"You did a great job, Mom. Don't be so hard on yourself. There are all kinds of bad influences kids must deal with. People at school, crap they see on TV, social media."

An exasperated sigh breathed through the phone.

"Look, Mom, I'll see what I can do. I don't have connections or anything, but maybe I can track her on social media. She lives on that stuff."

"Used to. I don't get all that Tumbler and Insta-whatever, but I checked her Facebook and don't see much going on there. It's like she just... disappeared."

"No one uses Facebook anymore, Mom. She probably made up a dummy account for your eyes only. Come on, get real. If Erin wants to cavort online, she'll find a way. Maybe I can outsmart her. It would probably help find her. Besides, the cops might be right. Even if she's doing drugs, she's probably just staying at a friend's house."

Her mother went into a fresh fit of crying. It took Amber a good ten minutes to calm her before she could hang up the phone. She knew Erin had dabbled with drugs. She tried to warn her younger sister about the pitfalls of addiction, but Erin was strong-willed. At least that was a nice way to explain her rebellious attitude towards just about everything. She was a bit of a punk rock girl, but Amber knew rebellion was her sister's way of making up for the things they lacked growing up. Erin was a sweet girl under the rough façade, but most people didn't know that. She kept a lot hidden.

By morning, Amber had her bags packed. The academy was scheduled to take a break in a week, but there was no time to waste. Her mother's heart was broken, Amber could hear it over the phone.

She knew too well that once someone was using, the choice to overcome addiction had to be one they made themselves. But it wouldn't stop Amber from doing everything she could to guide her sister in the right direction and get her the help she needed.

Besides, maybe things aren't that bad yet. If I get to her soon enough, maybe I can bring her around.

Amber should have known better, but she left the training facility and took a greyhound bus back to El Cajon, California.

CHAPTER 2

The house on Second Street looked like a goddamned junkie oasis. There were at least ten cars taking up residence in the front yard, overflowing from the driveway and sprinkling the dead grass like giant rusted carcasses, leaking blood-oil and scrapped parts. The house's windows were closed all the time, sunlight blotted out by heavy mismatched curtains. Some of the windows were boarded where glass had been broken when some sorry sack tried to break in. Some of them had large wood dowels pushed in diagonally so those particular windows couldn't be raised, which was overkill considering they were all screwed and nailed to the frames anyway. Garbage was piled on either side of the house in heaping, rat-infested hills; the foul depths of which buried many a secret. The place stood out in an aging neighborhood, hidden behind a wall of refuse and clutter, and yet people ignored their worst thoughts while passing by.

Kyle "Pizzo" Gaferty stood outside the front door. He took a deep breath before knocking. He'd been to other such places on many occasions, but it was always tense walking into one of the Queen's houses for something other than merely getting high.

A tiny, hinged lookout made of brass was embedded in the door. Opening, a grimy, squinted eye peered out. "Pizzo?"

"Yeah, man, it's me. Let me in."

"You got an appointment?"

"Yeah. Picking up some shit."

"Got money?"

"Just fucking' let me in, 'kay."

"You better have money or it's your ass. No one gonna bail you out in here, man."

"I'm cool, just let me in."

Pizzo's head darted around as if someone was following him, eyes scanning through the decrepit cars, toward the street. People drove by fast, many of the locals too used to seeing the trashed house to pay much attention to it anymore. It was an eyesore, better forgotten than be concerned about.

The deadbolt clicked, followed by no less than five other locks, and then the door opened. Pizzo slipped into the dank domain, immediately sickened and thrilled by the mélange of odors, foul and temptation: weed, whiskey, meth, grime, piss, spray paint. A television droned in a corner, fighting for audible dominance with a team of dust-caked ceiling fans and a boisterous conversation between several tweakers passing a glass pipe. They all eyed Pizzo, some with disdain, others out of curiosity. They were awful specimens. The kind of guys Pizzo told himself he would never become, only they looked worse for wear than the usual speed freaks he rubbed shoulders with.

The sneaky bastard who let Pizzo into the house wandered off down a hallway before Pizzo got a good look at him. It was hard to remember faces when they were all so strung out and the only time Pizzo saw these people was when he was high.

"Pizzo?" said one of the guys passing the pipe.

Pizzo didn't recognize the guy. "Yeah?"

The guy beamed, showing off a horrid case of meth mouth like he'd been gnawing on a handful of drywall screws. His nose was worn away, looking like the aftermath of melanoma. His skull gleamed though a thin layer of threadbare flesh stretched tight over his face. The hair was thin and sweaty and appeared to have been pulled out in clumps, leaving random bald spots dotted with scabs. Pizzo might have thought he had cancer and was going through chemo had the others not been in the same wasted state.

"It's Randy," the guy said.

Pizzo squinted his eyes. He whispered the man's name, scanning the cobwebbed banks of his mind to place the face.

The man spoke like he had marbles in his mouth. "Shit, man, Randy from Jimco Painting."

Pizzo contemplated. "Randy? That you? No shit."

Randy bobbed his head and looked like a sad jack o lantern. One of his cracked-out cronies passed the pipe.

"Hey!" came a voice from beyond a pair of French doors separating the living room from the family room. The man who stood there was a fucking monster. "You Pizzo?"

Pizzo nodded.

"C'mere."

Pizzo glanced at Randy, who was well-absorbed in the act of swirling a flame beneath the bowl of the pipe and decided against some kind of half-assed goodbye. He couldn't believe what Randy had turned into. They worked together only six months ago, both full-on speed freaks, and now this.

Pizzo approached the French doors. The edges where hands frequented to open and close them were black with grime and two of the panes were busted, repaired with duct tape and cardboard. The man at the doors was like Randy only worse for wear. His head was bald and malformed, lumpy like someone went to town with a baseball bat and the dude somehow came out of it alive. His eyes were off-centered, and his nose was completely gone, leaving gaping hollows dribbling bloody snot over his upper lip like sap from a scarred maple tree.

The man stared at Pizzo and nodded knowingly. "So, you're the one who's gonna introduce this stuff to the world?" His voice came out quick like a hummingbird in flight.

"It's already on the streets, man. At least, people are talking about it."

The man chuckled; a snort whistled out of the holes where his nose should have been. "Hard to keep this kind of secret. Goddamned tweakers want to tell everyone about the good shit they've been doing."

You're one to talk, Pizzo thought, as if he were one to talk considering his nickname and reputation.

A woman emerged from a door with an eight-ball spray-painted on it. Above the eight ball it said *NO DRAMA ROOM*. Had Pizzo not seen it, he wouldn't have believed it, but she was in worse shape than the man standing before him. Her face wasn't just destroyed and degenerated, but malformed, as if she had gone through some kind of lycanthropic transformation coming to a stop midrange. Her mouth extended like a snout, all red and sore looking, like maybe she scratched it too much. She approached the man Pizzo was speaking to and presented him with a small box. The man grabbed the box and the woman retreated into the room without a word.

No fucking drama.

The man set the box on a greasy-looking couch, then removed the lid. Inside was a huge bag of crystalline shards. It almost looked like a pile of broken frosted glass or thin sheets of ice chipped off a block.

"Here it is. We've got this shit going out all over town. Sell it just like regular speed, but remember, this stuff ain't normal. This shit'll fuck you up." He sniffed again, as if trying to gather up the snot running down his face. "Has a punch that really gets you in the gonads, bro. This stuff'll change the way junk-heads look at dope." The man's smile was psychotic at best. Frightening, really.

Pizzo nodded, silently admiring the huge bag of ice he was going to be leaving this tweaker pad with. The man opened the bag, pulling out a shard. He pushed around some debris then set the bag on the glass top of an end table. Using a razor blade, he crunched the meth then chopped it into a couple of powdery lines of fine, broken glass. The guy produced a small cut of straw out of nowhere and held it out to Pizzo. Knowing this was a test and considering Pizzo had never been to this house before, much less met this corroded junkie, he took the straw and sucked both lines up his nostrils with little hesitation.

The man lit a cigarette, inhaled deeply, and coughed. Smoke spewed out of his nostril holes like broken windows on a burning house. He used his thumb and forefinger to seal the Ziploc plastic bag.

"So, Dr. Scabs is trying something new. He wants you to sell this stuff and come back with the money." He took a drag.

"You don't come back with the money, someone will find you and rip your tongue out through your throat," he said with smoke in his lungs, all casual like. "I think they call that a *Columbian Necktie*, or something."

Pizzo nodded. His body rushed, feeling like he was in a fighter plane without the dome window, heading straight down for a Kamikaze landing. His sinuses throbbed and his teeth felt like Chicklets, and he couldn't feel much of his face anymore.

Smoke piled out of the man's nostrils. "Good shit, ain't it? Really grabs you by the short hairs and *pulls*, don't it?"

Pizzo felt a familiar sensation as if he could run around the room like the Flash and then suddenly his consciousness slammed back into his body, pulling him into to reality. "Yeah," he said lamely, heartbeat thrumming. He hadn't felt sensations quite like this since he'd first tried speed, and even then, it was watered down compared to how high he was at the moment.

The man extended the hefty bag of dope. "Take it. I expect you back by the end of the week. You come to me with the money. You can't find me, ask for Leche."

"How much do you expect?" Pizzo swallowed, but his mouth was too dry. He could barely speak. "What's this shit worth?"

"As long as you sell more than you pinch, we're good. Don't worry about a solid number. I'll know how well you did when I count the cash, got it?"

Pizzo didn't like the sound of that, but he grabbed the bag anyway, placing it into the backpack he slung over his shoulder when he walked in. "Really, man, how much money are you looking for? I don't want to come back here all short 'n' shit."

"You worry too much, bro. Get the fuck outta here and push the shit. That's what Scabs wants. He wants this stuff to be the new face of the addict. Meth that's stronger than meth, stuff so powerful crack cowers in its shadow. But I expect some money, and I'll be able to tell if you're dipping into the bag too much. Now fucking go. I'm already sick of looking at you."

Leche turned his back on Pizzo and walked away, slipping into the *NO DRAMA ROOM* where the malformed girl had gone. After a moment to catch his runaway brain, Pizzo left the house without so much as looking at the lounging tweakers, whores, and junkies with bad skin and even worse teeth.

Outside, he felt like he was in a whole new world. This new shit was far stronger than anything he'd ever put up his nose before. The stroll down the front walkway to his car seemed like an eternity. He saw things in the shadows, but every time he tried to focus on them, they fled. That was the kind of shit longtime addicts saw.

CHAPTER 3

The drive back to El Cajon from the central valley was spent on autopilot. The possibilities were very real that Amber's sister was nose deep in dangerous drugs. It was too easy to succumb to the pitfalls of drug abuse, especially in a town like El Cajon. There were bad influences everywhere, and there was no way for their mother to restrict Erin from hanging out with the kinds of kids who came from desperate or plain out negligent families, the types who grew up around dope and dabbled in pot when the kids with responsible parents were still thrilled with Saturday morning cartoons.

The other concern plaguing Amber's mind was whether she should make contact with her mother. How would her mother react? Amber worried she was taking a fool's chance even coming back like she could save Erin from her own damn mistakes. Things didn't always work out that way, and if the poor girl was addicted, she would resent Amber for intruding. One thing Amber learned going through NA and AA programs was that the addict wouldn't change until the addict was damn well ready. To force someone often made things worse.

And even with this knowledge, Amber went AWOL and rushed back to a town that would eat you up if you didn't watch out.

The decision to stay at a motel solidified as the car glided into the parking lot of a place Amber once knew in a life that seemed to have been lived in someone else's body. A past she tried to forget, but was forced to think about a lot during the trip back home.

The motel was a good thirty years outdated with deep cracks in the stucco and a giant sign in funky seventies font that read: *Midtown Motel*, though it was on east Main, which was a sort of skid row lined with similar two-story motels frequented by prostitution, drugs, lowlifes, and families fallen on hard times. People didn't stay in these places because they were passing through. If you stayed a day, you were getting high or turning a trick, otherwise you paid by the week. For many, a place like the Midtown Motel was a last stand before ending up on the streets.

The lobby smelled faintly of incense and grimy carpets that were steamed too many times rather than replaced. The clerk, a stick bug of a man with a drawn face and black beard with hints of gray, stood behind the desk, focused on his phone. If those eyes ever showed even a modicum of joy, that was stifled long ago, probably due to watching the daily refuse coming and going, forgetting decent people existed somewhere in this cruel world.

The clerk didn't say anything as Amber approached the counter. He put his phone down and stared at her as if he could communicate telepathically through sad eyes. Perhaps he remembered her. She was in much better health these days, had more meat on her bones and fewer lines on her face. He was judging her, that was for sure. This wasn't the kind of place for *hellos* and *how are yous*.

"I need a room," Amber said. "For a week, maybe longer."

"Cash or credit?"

"Credit."

The man pulled out a dinosaur of a credit

machine and slammed it on the scuffed counter. "You'll have to pay in advance."

Amber nodded.

"There's also a deposit, refundable when you return your keys."

"A deposit? What for?"

The desk clerk was writing up a receipt. His eyes rolled up to look at Amber. "You serious? Everyone asks for a deposit in El Cajon. You got to. People come in here and think they can live like animals and there's no recourse. Well, there is. If I gotta paint or repair carpet damage or replace a mattress, whatever, I keep the deposit. I don't make shit on the deposit, by the way. It's collateral. And most the time it doesn't cover the damage anyway. You want a room; you pay the deposit."

Amber shrugged. "Makes sense."

The clerk ran her card by slamming a lever on the antiquated hunk of metal, which made a carbon copy image of her credit card. It wasn't lost on her that this would be a ridiculously easy way for this guy to steal her identification, or at least make some grandiose purchases from the catalogues piled on the corner of the front desk.

"One key, right?" he asked.

Amber nodded. "Just me."

His eyes studied her a little closer. "Look, I don't turn business away, but you don't look like my average customer. You watch yourself." He turned and scanned an array of keys hanging on a board behind him. Amber couldn't remember the last time she stayed in a place that didn't use key cards. He produced a single oversized key. "You're in room 204, right side of the building, just up the stairs. Make sure you put the *DO NOT DISTURB* sign on your door unless you want the place cleaned. I have a lady, comes by everyday, but most folks like their privacy around here." He paused, his body sort of slumping. "My cleaning lady hasn't been coming by as much either." He leveled his eyes at Amber. "Things are getting so bad out there. You be careful, hear me."

Amber nodded. "I'll be fine, thanks."

He handed over the key, a receipt, and a small diagram of the building with room 204 circled.

Main Street was unassuming to the average *El Cajonian* driving by on their way to the supermarket or freeway. Everyone knew undesirables ruled the streets on bicycles and feet, and they all knew what went on in the motels, but over time everything blended into the background. The homeless were assumed deadbeats, drug addicts and losers, and the tweakers were just that: tweakers. Easy to gawk at from the confines of an air-conditioned car with the doors locked. Street level scum were as normal as the tides or a trip to the zoo.

Amber knew *this* world better than the people driving by. If they happened to see her walking from her car to the motel, would they assume she was scoring dope? No, they wouldn't even stop to consider what she was doing. They just drove on by. Being on street level like this made her invisible to the masses. Only the police would bat an eye, and even they wouldn't linger too long in their assumptions, not unless she was exhibiting odd behavior. Even then the cops often turned the other cheek. There were too many freaks to bother with the crazies, small-time pushers and users. Too much paperwork involved.

After retrieving her bag from the car, Amber headed across the faded asphalt parking lot to the staircase flanking the right side of the motel. She had only been in the academy for two months, and yet she found herself thinking as an officer. It would take hours on the job to really get the feel for police work, but she was already perceiving her surroundings differently. The weeds grew from cracks in the pavement, the overfilled dumpster nestled into a small fenced area with asphalt darkened by putrid juice, leaking from so much waste and drunkard urine, the old beater cars filling so few spaces in the parking lot, causing hers to look out of place, blinds flickering ever so slightly, as if someone were peeking through, or maybe paranoid out of their heads.

The unit below Amber's was the only one with an open door, a fan propped to pull out some of the hot air. Their AC unit must have been broken. As Amber passed by she glanced up, catching a set of eyes that had been watching her the entire time. Her glance was nothing more than that, nothing to cause suspicion, however what she saw brought forth a scream which she caught in her throat. The academy prepares officers-in-training for so much, but no one is ever ready for something like this.

Amber hesitated at the bottom of the stairs, hand on the worn, chipped black iron railing. The open door was visible between gaps in the concrete stairs. The fan hummed in the doorframe. The man she saw inside wasn't merely wasted away, he appeared to have barely survived an IED bombing and healing horribly. His mouth hung agape, most of the teeth gone. He had no lips, just poorly healed flesh and open sores, and the look he gave her, the eyes seemed to accuse her of something, perhaps being in the wrong place or maybe the fact she witnessed his scars.

Amber shuddered as she walked up the stairs. Gum stains decorated the steps in circles of black at such intervals they almost appeared to be in a purposeful pattern. The iron handrail shook with each delicate step, causing a faint metallic rattle. At the top, she took a few steps and found room 204. Her key glided into the lock. She opened the door and turned to look out at the parking lot before entering. The man in the room below was halfway across the parking lot, heading for the sidewalk along Main Street. He paused, turned, looked up at her, and then continued on his way.

Amber closed the door and locked it.

The room was just as outdated as the front office, furniture mismatched and paintings on the walls of landscapes and fruit in whitewashed frames. The television was a flatscreen, surprisingly enough, and the sign outside boasted of FREE HBO and WiFi, which would certainly come in handy. The receipt she'd been given had the WiFi password. The carpet had clearly been shampooed enough times to pull threads out here and there, but stubborn stains came back like the ghosts of some sordid past. The wallpaper peeled at some of the seams, and there was a yellowed drywall patch around the light switch next to the door.

After an exhaustive search of the mattress for bedbugs, Amber figured the desk clerk must have had mercy on her by giving her one of the best rooms in the place. The lack of bedbugs was downright suspicious, but in the best of ways. Amber had been chewed up by bedbugs in the past at similar dives, but she couldn't go back to that, not even for the sake of her sister. There were other motels to choose from if it came to that. Also, there weren't any roaches, which could have been due to her room being on the second floor. Whatever the reason, she decided that staying there for a while would suffice. She had enough money for a few months, but that was it. If Amber couldn't find her sister and do her best at saving the poor girl in that amount of time, then her efforts would have been futile.

After a trip to the local market for some provisions, Amber found an old map of San Diego in the lobby of the motel on a rack full of little pamphlets for Sea World, the world-famous San Diego Zoo, Balboa Park and other such local tourist traps. The rack was thick with dust and Amber figured any coupons were probably years expired.

Back in her room, she used pins to tack the map upon the wall. She used one of the drawers in the dresser to store her snacks, tried to fill the ice bucket for the warm soda she bought, but found it out of order. Finally, she began scouring the Internet for information that would give her some kind of lead to work on.

There were several local stories about some new drug craze that seemed to work at an alarming pace destroying people twice as fast as meth. Some people were calling it Super Speed, others called it Craze, but the most distinguishable name for this super dope was Tweak, which had always been a slang term for meth as far as Amber knew.

After locating a pad of notepaper (the type that usually had the name of the motel, though, in this case, it had the name of a local real estate mogul), Amber used the pen, which *did* have the motel's name, and wrote the word *TWEAK* in large block letters. She tacked it on the wall above the map.

Is this crazy?

No doubt the academy would be contacting her. It was amazing her phone hadn't been blowing up. Maybe they didn't care. Maybe this sort of thing happened all the time. Weak people who couldn't cut it, who didn't have the chops to serve the community. It wasn't *that* hard, really. Nothing like what she'd heard about military boot camp. She would have completed her training had she stayed, but going AWOL pretty much put a nix on her future in law enforcement. That kind of thing was frowned upon no matter what the reason.

Amber looked at the word *TWEAK* on the wall and thought of Erin.

She grabbed the ashtray provided (no motel logo) and went outside for a smoke. She stood on the landing, holding the small ashtray in one hand and managing the cig in the other. It was the only vice that stuck with her after getting sober a few years back. A small price, as far as she was concerned. Some people considered nicotine a drug, but that was crazy. She vaguely remembered getting a buzz off the first cigarette she smoked, but that was a long time ago, and that sort of thing never happened again. If you didn't get a high off a substance, how was it a drug?

Because you're addicted, bitch.

Amber took a drag. She scanned the riffraff walking Main Street, slogging along like extras on set for a zombie movie, heads held low, shuffling around like they were on their last hope. One guy rode by on a rat bike. Back in the day before she dabbled with dope, Amber and her friends called them *TOABs* (pronounced like toad, the slang stood for Tweaker on a Bike). The bicycle was the tweaker's most valuable commodity since most of them had long ago crashed whatever car they had been driving when they dived into slow degeneration of heavy drugs, or they sold their car to buy drugs. Bikes were easy to steal; fun to take apart and put back together during a drug frenzy, which was therapeutic when your mind was going a million miles an hour.

The guy on a bike had a mustache sideburn

combo (popular with the TOABs) and was riding without holding the handlebars, arms crossed. He wore greasy clothes, hair longish and dirty like he used wet gravel for shampoo. His head moved around as if fixed on a swivel, and when he took an extended look at the motel (looking for someone specific) Amber saw that his nose was also gone, eyes so deep set they looked like gaping hollows.

Amber recoiled and dropped her cigarette.

"Shit!"

She peered over the railing. The smoldering cancer stick lay on the faded blacktop below, a tendril of smoke rising. Amber looked up and the TOAB was gone, replaced by an old man with a bag of groceries. She looked down and gasped. The man from the room below was bent over. He grabbed her cig, straightened himself, and looked up.

Amber felt frozen in her skin, staring at this man whose face was worn away around the mouth and nose. She could see his brown teeth, gnarled like twisted tree roots. He opened his mouth and put the cig between his lips, making a sickening sucking noise as he pulled in a drag. She swore he grinned, though it was hard to tell, and then smoke seemed to erupt from his face, drifting through the hollow nose holes, between the ragged teeth and through little gaps in torn cheeks.

Nausea washed over Amber. She turned and rushed into her room, locking the door behind her.

CHAPTER 4

Pizzo had no trouble unloading the dope. In fact, he was shocked at how easy it was. Once word got out that he had the Crazy Tweak he couldn't beat the junkies off with a stick.

He sat in his car in the back of a gas station down the street from the house on Second Street. He had a load of cash and was nervous about delivering. *Was it enough?* He didn't want a Columbian Necktie, that was for sure.

Jacking the seat back into a more relaxing position, Pizzo sighed and put a hand over his eyes, rubbing his temples. *How the hell had he gotten himself into this?* He wanted to start his own drywall business and was in no financial, or even physical shape to get a loan. He figured selling some speed was about the only thing he could do to make a quick buck outside of winning the lottery or robbing a bank. And he made a good pull from this first pound of meth, but how much of the cash was his? Any of it? He wasn't going to do someone's dirty work and get nothing in return. He was living out of a goddamned car, for crying out loud. What did Leche and this Dr. Scabs guy want from him?

"Fuckin' Ronnie."

Pizzo had been clean and sober for about six months, which was a goddamned feat considering how much speed he used to smoke. Didn't earn his nickname for nothing. He was doing good, but then he lost his job after the company didn't win a big bid on a tract home development that was supposed to take them though the rest of the year. Pizzo was already struggling with the debts he'd accumulated when he was using. Unable to get a job with another contractor, he found himself too prideful to go back to slinging burgers and bagging fries. *Better than living in a car.*

Pizzo poured sweat like his car was a sauna. He chewed on the inside of his cheeks, a nervous junkie twitch he'd developed when he was using. He'd knocked it off until— The chewing escalated. The inside of his cheeks was ragged and sore, but he couldn't even feel the pain when his tongue flicked pieces of shredded skin which sometimes got caught between his teeth.

The last remnants of the Crazy Tweak dotted the center of a well-crumpled rip of tin foil. Just enough to get him though this drop off.

He angrily chewed the soft, mushy flesh of his inner cheek; spit out a piece of wet, bloody skin.

Oh, why did that malformed fucker at the Second Street house force him to have a hit? Pizzo hadn't intended on taking the drugs, he just wanted to sell the stuff. That was always a hard concept for him to understand, but plenty of his hookups were strictly dealers, preferring to sit down with a cocktail at the end of the night, maybe some weed. Big Man Brando used to tell him it was unwise of the pusher to sample the product. Bad for business. That always stuck with Pizzo. It was going to be his model, and he was only going to sell until he had enough to buy a van and equipment he needed for the drywall business.

The last remnants of dope found their way into the bowl of a well-blackened glass pipe. It was automatic. Pizzo wasn't even thinking about it anymore. Just did it. He flicked a flame to life and swirled it under the glass. Once a tendril of smoke rose, he sucked on the stem.

As his mind exploded with a rush of sensation, the shadow figures made themselves clearer. He'd been seeing them more frequently, and they were in abundance at the Second Street house. On one hand they frightened him, and then on the other he kind of liked them. Seeing the shadow people was a sure sign the dope was good and strong. He was feeling lost without their presence.

There was another problem.

Chew. Spit.

Now that he tried the Crazy Tweak, he needed more.

***

Leche came out of the NO DRAMA ROOM with an old cigar box in hand. Behind him, two shadow people came out and sort of dissipated into the ether.

"What have you got for me?" Leche asked. His face looked like someone doused him in battery acid, but Pizzo wasn't fazed, not after dealing with the new wave of junkies on the streets of El Cajon.

Pizzo, seated on a couch, opened his backpack and pulled out a black plastic bag. He set the bag on top of a littered coffee table. He looked up at Leche like he was making some kind of offering. The faint outline of shadow people loomed over Leche, as if they were also inspecting the load of cash.

"How much?" Leche asked. He set the cigar box down, scratched his head. Some hair came out. Too much hair.

"About four." Pizzo nibbled his cheek.

"Four?"

"Grand."

Leche nodded. Scratched his head. His fingers

came back with red tips. "Good shit, right?" He grinned, which looked grotesque. Men with such horrid disfigurements didn't smile. "Not bad." Leche nodded in approval. "You didn't pinch too much. You don't even know what I had to do to this guy Brando."

Brando?

"Fucker came back with eight bills, man. You believe that shit? Had too many excuses. He pinched too much for personal use or gave it to his friends or whatever."

Leche scratched his head. Hairs clung to blood-wet fingertips.

"What'd you do to him?"

"That's for me to know and you to wonder. You did good, Pizzo. You don't have to see what happened to Brando. Not today. Hopefully not ever. Now look, you take the cash. Get yourself a room. You've been selling out of your car and that's kind of risky."

Pizzo narrowed his eyes. "How did you know that?"

"Dr. Scabs has eyes all over this town, ese." Leche scratched his head and twitched violently. The shadow figures that loomed over him were gone. "That cash is enough for a room. Plenty. Here's another pound." He opened the cigar box and pulled out a bag of shards. "Sell it. Get it out there. Come back to me with the cash. Easy."

Pizzo nodded, chewed the inside of his cheek, swallowing the tiny bits of flesh on his tongue. "What about the left-over money?" He picked up the black bag of cash and deposited it in his backpack. "This is more than enough for a room."

"Living expenses. Get yourself a gun if you don't already have one. And who fucking works for free, right? I'll take a cut from the next batch."

Leche stood, hand back at the side of his head, where his finger was inserted, as if he were scratching his brain. He twitched again like his probing finger hit a sensitive spot or a nerve or something. "See you in a few days." He walked away, slipping into the NO DRAMA ROOM. There were no shadow people, which was a sure sign Pizzo needed more Crazy Tweak.

Pizzo slammed the bag of dope into his backpack. He walked through the French doors in the middle of the house, heading for the door. In the front room a motley gathering of junkies and freaks were getting high. Pizzo glanced at them, and then did a double take. He kind of recognized the guy from work, but he was in bad shape, as were all of them. Like their flesh was melting away, piece by piece.

They just sort of stared at Pizzo as he passed, eyes long and dark in faces like wax dummies on a red-hot potbelly stove, only worse. Pizzo didn't get but a glance, he was too scared to stare longingly, but he swore some of them were deformed, as if the skulls behind the taut, torn up flesh had somehow changed shape.

Pizzo headed to Magnolia Avenue. There was a particular motel there that had tweakers like the sewers have rats. The room rates would be cheap, and he would be able to unload the pound of meth without a hitch.

CHAPTER 5

—–—

The walls were decorated with random items such as worn T-shirts with goofy sayings to old rock posters (one was a fuzzy black light poster of Ozzy Osbourne from the *Diary of a Madman* album) to, of all things, potato chip bags.

The place would have been strange to Erin only a year ago, but she could hardly remember how she even got there in the first place. Had she driven? Walked? How long had she been there?

A trembling hand slid across a clammy face. Her limbs hardly felt like her own, almost as if they were individual entities. Her face was heavy like a mask. She was tempted to pick at her cheek, just to see if it was made of foam or latex or whatever. Surely not skin. It wasn't her face, right?

Erin heard of the bugs. She'd seen addicts picking at their skin, talking about maggots, but she had never seen anything like that. Not yet. That was her barometer. *Just so long as I'm not seeing bugs.* She'd check herself into rehab if ever she saw the bugs. That was a promise.

But goddamn did she want to get the mask off her face. The latex. She absentmindedly picked at her cheek. If she could just get her fingernail under the mask, she could peel it away from her skin.

The door opened. Erin's head shot up like her neck was spring loaded. A man walked in. Erin's eyes grew in her head. Was it a man? *Am I trippin'?*

"You're Erin, right?" His voice was a reflection of his ghastly appearance.

Erin nodded. Picked at her face. She eyed the morsel. Funny how the latex was red and wet.

"You're here to see Scabs, right?" He breathed heavily, unable to close his mouth since he no longer had lips. His skull attempted to break away from the prison of his face. Looked painful, but he didn't seem to notice.

"Yeah," Erin said sort of dreamily. She'd completely forgotten why she was there, almost as if she had been drugged... well, as if someone drugged her. She'd been drugging herself for quite a while now. Too long for her to even remember where the hell she'd come from. She'd spent weeks, if not months in some foggy timeframe like living in the Twilight Zone.

"Good." The fiend hissed. He picked at the jagged, crusty skin around his elongated skeletal mouth. "Yeah, good, real good. I'll get Dr. Scabs. He's here. You won't regret this, I swear." His speech was erring on the devotional, like Scabs was Christ himself. "I envy you. I wish I could..." Anger entered those eyes, those human eyes in the face of a monster. He turned and left the room.

While Erin waited for Dr. Scabs, she smoked some speed. It was the new Crazy Tweak stuff that had been circulating, and boy was it good. The inhale was cool, like a super strength menthol cigarette, and it went right to your head. *Zap!* Thundering heart. Blood pumping through her veins like the blood cells were transformed into miniature jet planes, coursing through her body along some intricate track and breaking mach speed. The big hit was a supernova, a sonic boom exploding within every fiber of her molecular structure.

This dope was better than sex, and that wasn't hyperbole. Erin didn't need a man if she had this shit. She didn't need anything.

Not even her family.

Not even her mother.

How Erin's mother could seep into her head was astonishing. Even the best drugs couldn't erase the past, not forever at least. After Erin ran away from home, she pretty much forgot about the life she once lived, the childish impulses she'd felt towards stupid boys, the boring pop music and drab chitchat with girlfriends. They were probably stuck with asshole, hipster boyfriends planning some white picket life. Fuck that. Erin had everything she could want in the resin-stained bowl of a glass pipe.

From her peripherals, she saw the shadow people emerging. They'd frightened her at first, a sure sign she was close to seeing those damn bugs on her skin that she so feared, but they mostly just watched her, flickering in and out of her vision. They were there all the time now. Hiding behind the furniture, poking their heads through the walls like ghosts. Sometimes that's what Erin thought they were. Ghosts.

She took another hit. Picked at the latex. Or was it rubber?

The pipe took away her fears. The pipe gave her the best sensations. The pipe never lied.

The pipe was always there for her.

Always.

Not like her sister, leaving for the Police Academy of all things. The fucking POLICE! How could she do that? Amber had known the pipe. She may have quit, but how the hell do you find yourself teaming with the enemy, with the pigs? Amber joining the force was worse than leaving Erin alone with their neurotic mother.

Oh, what a twisted world it would be if her sister came bursting through the door, part of some

NARC force, there to bust any given dope house Erin chilled in. Push everyone out like roaches, make some arrests and search the premises for drugs, guns and meth lab materials. And there Erin would be, yanked out by her own flesh and blood.

The thought made her sick. Made her reaffirm what she was doing with her life.

She examined the pipe, tracing the black swirls of the bowl with her eyes. The secrets of life were in there somewhere. Yep, the pipe wouldn't hurt her.

The pipe never lied.

Long live the pipe!

Mornings when she woke and didn't have any drugs, her stomach hurt and her head ached, she cursed her mother for driving her to this. On those mornings she could see the addiction and it hurt. She wanted it gone, away, but the only solution, the only thing she understood was using. When you're an alcoholic it was called the hair of the dog that bit you. Sounded kind of nice. When you're a junkie it was just called using. Feeding the monkey on your back. But damn, once the monkey is fed, it all comes clear. The shadow people came out to greet her, all devilish smiles and flickering like silent movie stars. The answers were in the pipe.

The answers were ruining her teeth.

The answers were causing her to peel the mask off her face. *As long as there are no bugs, you don't have a problem, bitch.*

The answers...

The door opened again. A man walked in, closing the door behind him. He was different from the last guy in that his face wasn't malformed, yet he was equally hideous due to the odd texture of his skin. He wore a crisp lab coat that looked so out of place in a dump like this, it added to the strangeness he exuded.

"I hear you want to see me," he said.

His eyes blazed white from a face that had normal shape, yet was caked with something of a crust like dried mud or...

Scabs?

Erin nodded.

"You want to help the cause, is that it?"

Erin nodded again. "Yes."

The man stepped forward. She could see his grotesque face clearer, and it was worse than the others, worse than the men she'd been seeing who seemed to be melting. His entire face was covered in layers of scabs like the crust on chicken fried steak.

"Don't be scared," he said. The scabs around his mouth cracked as he spoke. "I'm a doctor."

CHAPTER 6

Seeking out Erin's friends proved to be more exhausting than Amber expected. The days of phone directories and rolodexes might have been over, but the internet didn't necessarily make things much easier.

One thing Amber found out rather quickly was about three months ago Erin had completely fallen off social media. About the time Amber left for the academy. Coincidence? Amber thought about that. The Police Academy wasn't forever. Erin knew her sister would be back. Amber remembered the comments Erin made in the weeks leading to her leaving for the academy. *Off to join the pigs?* Sometimes Erin would put her hand over her mouth and nose, breathing deep like Darth Vader: *You're going to the Dark Side.* Erin was a horror and sci-fi junkie, so it was no surprise to Amber when her Vader impression ended with Pinhead: *We have such sights to show you.*

The closer Amber came to what her sister dubbed D-Day; the more Erin dropped hurtful comments. She'd walk into Amber's room and sniff a few times: *Smells like bacon.* Erin tried to laugh it all off, but it hurt her deep inside, and now she wondered if she had been too preoccupied with her own path in life to recognize that her little sister was following in her footsteps. It wasn't all the police bashing comments, necessarily, but that Amber seemed to forget, or perhaps neglect, to love her family, to show compassion. Erin wasn't a heartless girl by any stretch of the imagination, but in those weeks before Amber left, her behavior changed drastically. Drugs did that to a person. There's a certain *zombification*. Amber knew this from personal experience.

After finding some of Erin's friends on Instagram and sending them messages, Amber left the motel room to get a coffee and some fresh air. Well, as fresh as could be in a town like El Cajon.

The air was choke-worthy and the coffee burnt. But what did Amber expect from a donut shop on Main Street? The pot probably hadn't been changed since late morning, just sitting there on the heating pad, burning its way into a thick sludge. Amber drank it anyway.

A place like El Cajon doesn't change much in six months. Sitting in a window booth, Amber watched as people walked by, mostly homeless or destitute, dragging ass like they were on the verge of giving up. A close eye could recognize the prostitutes. They didn't look like what you saw in movies or crime dramas. They didn't wear skimpy outfits, high heels, and bright lipstick. They were addicts, looking for a hustle so they could powder their noses, some of them. Others were beholden to unseen pimps, watching from cars, keeping tabs, expecting money. About five years ago, El Cajon was caught in a massive prostitution sting covering several states and even branches in the UK and Amsterdam. A whole host of men and women alike had been enslaving girls as young as ten, forcing them on the streets. They often recruited from schools in poverty-stricken neighborhoods, promising money but delivering only pain and suffering. For a while there the problem seemed to have been largely eradicated. Locals were more vigilant if they saw something, but in a small city such as this one, littered with such hopelessness on the streets, it was only a matter of time before it all went to pot once again.

The prostitute stood close to a freeway off ramp. She wore yoga pants with tennis shoes and a stained white t-shirt with the bottom tied in a knot, Amber assumed was a desperate attempt at looking sexy. A black girl, hair dyed platinum blonde, but the dye job couldn't compete with her natural color, so she ended up with an orange, frizzy poof. She moved in a jagged sort of twitchy way indicating her preference for meth over other such recreational drugs as cocaine or heroin. After the big prostitution ring had been busted, the modern working girls were on their own, just trying to make a few bucks so they could get a fix. At least that was what Amber was to believe.

Amber wondered what she would have done if she were a police officer. Would she arrest the woman? How could she? She didn't even have probable cause. It wasn't illegal to make a fool of oneself in public, just so long as you weren't harming anyone. There was no way for Amber to prove she was a hooker. Or a junkie, for that matter. Such labels certainly seemed to applied.

A cop car drove by. Amber kept a keen eye on the officer. His head didn't so much as swivel in the direction of the tweaker prostitute. There was Amber's answer. Cops were used to this kind of thing. They were immune to it. Just another junkie. What were they going to do anyway? Busting the user was more paperwork than it was worth and didn't do a damn thing at solving the real issue. On top of that, there were countless women like Little Miss Twitch, enough to keep an officer busy all day if he stopped every one of them. Better to just roll on by. Ignore it. Pretend they didn't exist.

But how long could the law pretend? How much could they bat their eyes at?

One of Erin's friends messaged Amber:

Erin dropped out of school I thnk

Dunno

Don't talk to her anymore She started usin drugs hangin out w/ weirdos

That was it. No help at all.

Deciding she was going to have to look deeper, Amber went back to the hotel where she could use her laptop. On each tab she had another social media website with her sister's profile page. Instagram, Facebook, Twitter, SnapChat. All the sites she was familiar with. She made a timeline, jotted down names, went to their profiles, scratched off some names, circled others. If only she could get access to Erin's private messages.

Amber rubbed her eyes. At this point the coffee wasn't even working. She'd been at the computer like it was a job she was paid to do. She took a deep breath, focusing on the sheet of paper in hand. Most of the names she'd scrawled on there were scratched out. A teacher once told her that one line was enough to cross off a word or sentence, but Amber preferred to scratch the fucker out of existence. She didn't even want to see the name for fear of confusion.

Therefore, the paper in her hand smelled heavily of ink and was wavy from scratch marks.

How long had she been at it? An hour? Four?

Her eyes circled the one name that had yet to be scratched out.

Larry Hiriam.

How many hours did she have left in her this evening? Was it worth going into deeper internet searches? Amber knew the pitfalls of fatigue. In the movies people burned the midnight oil researching.

They had to. It pushed the plot forward. But she was exhausted and feared she might miss something important.

But she did find the man whose name now flashed in her mind in bright red fluorescent. She found him on Tinder (where he had apparently found Erin), and a simple Google search and a few bucks found her his mug shot.

CHAPTER 7

———

Larry Hiriam found himself on dope pickup duty again, only he didn't have a car and no one at the Second Street house was willing to drive him. Lousy tweakers sat around all day rotting their brains with the new super meth shit. Larry was smarter than that. He saw what it was doing to them. All those toxic chemicals just rotting their faces away right before their eyes and they didn't even have a damn clue. Or they didn't care.

Addiction is an angry bitch, always ready to slap you across the face and make you come back for more.

"C'mon, Red, gimme a ride. I'm just goin' down to the strip mall."

Red made an obnoxious slurping sound as he attempted to collect the bodily fluids oozing out of his melting face. He still had lips, though they were most certainly next on the chopping block. Larry watched the progression. It started with the nose and cheeks. It looked like Red had been on the losing side of a chemical disaster, like a car battery exploded in his face and etched his flesh away. A real-life Incredible Melting Man.

"No way, man," Red said, making a noise as he sucked air through gooey nostrils in the muck of his face. "I'm not going anywhere."

"Fuck, man. Seriously? Help a brother out, dude. I've got to pick up a load. I don't want to ride a bike. Too risky. Anyway, how the fuck are you going to get high if I don't get the stuff back here?"

Red considered this. His jaundiced eyes scanned the room, unable to stop on any one thing, unable to properly focus. He trained those googly orbs on Larry.

"I'll get you some right off the top," Larry said. "How's that sound?"

"Alright, man. C'mon."

They drove down Second Street about five miles to an abandoned strip mall once bustling with restaurants, bars, and chain stores. Behind the strip was an alley separating it from a series of dilapidated apartments. Red drove his car into a converted loading dock, concealed from the prying eyes of the police. There were a few other cars in the loading dock, as well as motorcycles and a pair of desperately abused individuals who seemed to prop one another up in a corner, perhaps drunk and stoned. Wasted. Indisposed.

Nothing new.

Red cut the engine. "I'm waiting here."

Larry raised his eyebrows. "The hell you are. You're comin' with me."

"I ain't going in there. No way, no sir. Fuck that noise, Jackson. This is a Hag House."

"Ain't no house."

"You know what I mean."

"Afraid of the Hags?"

"I've heard things."

Larry cocked a shyster's grin. "What have you heard?"

Red picked at the mess of his face. "Well, I heard the Hags eat people."

"That right? No shit, huh?" Red nodded. Larry said, "They're just drug queens, that's all. They don't eat people. They're the biggest dealers this side of the Southern border. That's all. Now quit acting like a little bitch and get out of the fucking car. I've got to bring this shit back to Second Street House, but I'll get someone else to give me a ride if I have to, and I won't be giving you shit, get it?"

Red groaned, picked at his face. "Aw, fuck. Okay."

The car doors echoed off the walls of the loading dock. The men walked through a large doorway, pushing through strips of thick plastic into what once served as a prescription drug store (some things never change). Immediately they were accosted by a tall man whose face looked like a bad makeup job for an extra in a zombie flick. Where the skin had rotted away the remaining muscle tissue sort of became glossed over with dried plasma like a new face emerging. It looked painful, but most of the men suffering such afflictions didn't seem to mind. It was probably wild amounts of drugs keeping them from feeling the pain of what was happening to their bodies.

"Who the fuck are you?" the zombie asked.

"I'm Larry. Here to pick up a load, man."

Zombie's eyes shifted to Red. "Who's this?"

"Red. Gave me a ride over here."

"You were supposed to come alone, weren't you?"

Larry smirked. "You don't want me walking or riding a bike, right? My understanding is that I'm picking up quite a load. They're completely dry over at Second Street House. If time is money, you all are fucking losing some goddamn money, aren't you?"

"It was only supposed to be you." Zombie was becoming more agitated, twitching and picking his skin. Just like all of them. All of the dope zombies. "Do you understand where you are? This isn't a fucking joke. This is the real shit, man." Zombie looked around nervously. "You best get out of here,

Red. I don't want to see you here again unless you're *told* to come here. And not by some fucking mule like Larry, but by one of the house bosses or a Hag or something."

"S'cuse me," Larry piped in. "Red's my ride, dude. The fuck?"

Zombie grabbed Larry's throat with hands splotchy with what looked like a bad skin disease, like tissue that was going necrotic. "Don't you fucking talk to me like that!"

A popping sound issued, more sudden than startling, and then Red's body collapsed. Zombie let go of Larry's throat, retracting his hand and stepping back defensively. Larry, confused and relieved that his windpipe wasn't being squeezed like a redneck on an empty beer can, stared at the newcomer holding a pistol with a homemade silencer affixed to the barrel (what looked like duct tape and PVC pipe).

Red bled out onto the concrete floor the way a spilled gallon of milk does. Blood gushed with the final pumps of his heart.

The newcomer pointed the gun at Larry. "You were supposed to come alone."

Larry nodded as if he was getting the picture, trying to assert himself. That man with the gun was unmistakable, even if Larry had only heard about him at various dope houses. You can't mistake a man whose skin is covered with scabs. "I needed a ride. Didn't know it would be such an issue." Larry glanced at Red. His hair was glossy black like he used enough gel to create an impenetrable crust.

"Soon it won't matter, but for now I have to cover my ass." Scabs tapped Red's leg with his foot, jiggling the body like a man cast in thick gelatin. "Guy like him finds out about this place and he's liable to come back. Best to just take him out right now." Scabs pointed his gun at Larry. "As for you..."

Larry's hands went up. "Whoa, look, Doc, you don't gotta worry about me."

"I don't even fucking know you. I trust my house bosses and who they send to me. This bleeding pile of shit wasn't sent to me." Scabs looked at Zombie and nodded his head toward Larry. "This the guy?"

Zombie nodded. "He supplies Second Street House."

"Second Street House." Scabs nodded. "How are things over there?"

"Good, I guess. I don't really hang around there. Just make deliveries, sell some of this shit."

Scabs nodded. "Yeah? And how are sales?"

Larry snickered. "I can't keep this shit stocked. Everyone wants a hit. Nobody wants the old shit. Fucking turn their noses up at regular meth. Doesn't do it for them anymore."

"That's good. That's what I want." Scabs itched the side of his cheek, releasing a small chunk of scab hanging off his face like a dry oatmeal cookie. He picked the piece off his cheek and stuck it in his mouth. Scabs nodded. "This is good. Very good." Scabs eyed Larry more closely. "But what about you? You into this stuff?"

Larry hesitated. He'd avoided taking the super meth, fooling one of the house bosses by switching out a rock with some shitty crystal he bought from some guys who were unconnected with the underground. He saw what the shit did to people, and it was fucking scary. "Yeah, I hit it sometimes, but I sell way more than I use."

Scabs didn't look convinced. "It's important you reserve some for yourself." To Zombie he said, "Where's that fucking guy, what's his name? Fucking Snaggletooth or something?"

"Snaggle?"

"Yeah. Gather him and some of the others. Load up the car."

Larry whistled and raised his eyebrows. "Load up the car? Just how much of this shit are we talking about?"

"You said it's going fast, which I suspected it would once it caught on. Remember crack? Back in the eighties?" Larry nodded. "That shit was so fucking addicting it ruined communities." He smiled, blood glistening between cracking scabs. "Made a lot of people rich."

"This stuff the new crack? Is that it?"

Scabs shook his head. "No, not really. It's different. Oh, it'll fuck up a community, that's for sure, but in an entirely different way. I'm not in it to get rich either."

"So how much are you sending me off with? I don't want to get popped on my way back, you know?"

"At least twenty, forty pounds, maybe more."

"Forty pounds! Fuck that shit. I'll be put away for life."

Scabs itched his arm. Blood seeped through the pristine white fabric where he'd broken through the armor of scabbing near his elbow. "You better drive carefully. And watch out for people on the streets. They can smell this stuff."

"What? Smell it? You out of your mind?"

Several characters came out of the murk pushing dollies on which were packages of dope wrapped tightly in cellophane. A lot of them.

"Nope," said Larry. "Uh huh. Not gonna do it. Too fucking risky."

As the men with the dollies came closer, Larry could see there was something wrong with them. They were thin like unwrapped mummies, alabaster skin red from itching, picking and scratching. The skin rotted or been picked clean from their faces, which resembled red, wet skulls with gleaming jaundiced eyes and gaping, empty maws like an infant's. Fingers clutching dolly handles were elongated, as if extra bones had developed, or perhaps the existing bones stretched. One of the trio belched out a groan and licked his drippy raw-skinned chops as he stared at Larry. There was something primal in the eyes that frightened Larry, but he did his best to hide his fear.

"In the car," Scabs said. "Keys?" he said to Larry.

"Probably unlocked, but I don't have the keys. Red's car."

"Red?" Scabs laughed. "He sure as hell is. You better get down there and find those keys."

Larry trembled. "I can't take the load. That's way more than forty pounds. Those are fucking twenty pounds apiece."

"All the better."

"Fuck it, I'm leaving."

"I'll have a bullet in the back of your skull before you get five feet." Larry stopped, but didn't turn around. "Better, I'll blow your kneecaps from behind and let *them* have some fun with you. They're getting used to the changes their bodies are undergoing. Wouldn't hurt for them to have something to play with."

The trio reentered the loading area after stocking Red's car with Crazy Tweak. They were so wasted away, and yet there was something about them that was truly terrifying. Something off about the shape of their heads, and those toothless wet mouths.

"I have a better idea, Larry. That's your name, right? Larry?"

Larry turned to face Dr. Scabs and nodded.

"Snaggle here's real handy with just about anything," Scabs said. "You know how it is with tweakers, always fixing shit, repairing stuff, taking it apart and doing it all over again. Snaggle is handy as fuck, as they say." Scabs itched, popped a fresh chunk in his mouth. "How about you boys make something real nice out of ol' Red here? You think you can do that? Show Mister Larry here that I mean business," Scabs' voice rose as he looked Larry in the eyes, "and I will not have someone fucking with my business, because I have eyes everywhere, Larry. I have eyes coming out my ass, and I see everything clearly now that the rain is gone. I can see for miles and miles and miles, and if you even have a wet dream about fucking with my operation, you'll have Snaggle here knocking on your door, or maybe Tool over there or Dave or fucking Gary or Jimbo or whoever the fuck." He fell strong on the K in fuck, really kicking it out from the back of his throat.

Scabs walked away, scratching his arms and face. Mumbling. Furious.

Before the goons could get to Red's body Larry knelt down and pick-pocketed the guy, careful not to get too much blood on his hands, and extricated the keys. After wiping his hands on Red's pants, Larry stepped back, wary of the slobbering goons who clearly became excited by the prospect of having a corpse to play with.

The goons looked at the body and then at each other, nodding and grunting and snickering as well as they could without lips. Their tongues filled the voids of their mouths like fat worms, twisting and turning, licking red gums, prodding the soft, puffy holes where teeth once were. They looked into one another's eyes with a lover's intensity, nodding as if communicating telepathically. One of them jetted off in search of something handy while the other two hefted the body away from the pool of coagulating blood. They flipped it over and stripped Red of his clothes.

Larry watched, unsure if he should leave just yet. Did Scabs want him to see what these freaks were going to do with the body? As some sort of warning?

After the clothes were torn away, one of the goons grabbed the man's cock and balls with both hands, sinking his elongated, twiggy fingers into the soft flesh at the very insides of Red's hairy thighs like oozing them into moldy cheese.

Larry cringed, doing everything he could not to yelp like a little bitch. These animals wouldn't take kindly to a little bitch. They probably ate little bitches for breakfast.

After sinking his fingers in deep, the goon grabbed on tight, folds of testicular skin and coarse hairs squeezing through his spindly digits. He then twisted to the left and to the right, just a half an inch each way, like easing out a giant cork. He gritted his teeth together into a serious death's-head grin and pulled, yanking Red's genitalia from the vortex of his thighs. Some of his insides were extracted, clinging to his sex organ. His body was fresh enough to bleed, though the release was more due to gravity than anything. Nothing spurted, which clearly displeased the goons considering the glimmer of emotion shown with the mottled skin around their roadmap eyes.

Larry gripped the keys so tight he could feel them pushing his skin to the breaking point. He was petrified to even move for fear they would rediscover his presence and give him a wicked knob job or worse. Fuck, they were upset about this one.

They might like to see the gusher erupting from ripping off a *live* man's rod.

The goon who left returned with a length of PVC pipe that was about two inches in diameter. The goon with a bloody dick in his hand as well as his counterpart nodded their approval. One freak grabbed the corpse and pulled the head back, yanking on the jaw like a sword swallower ready for a performance. The PVC pipe was crammed into the gaping pie-hole with care and junkie precision, eased down the larynx and throat until it became stuck. The freak clenched his teeth pushing harder as the others held the corpse tight. The pipe sunk more, then stuck again, then was pushed with more force, probably tearing through now-defunct organs. Soon enough, it managed to be guided through the corpses torso, popping out from its bloody pelvis.

Larry, clutching the keys in a white-knuckled fist, glanced at the car, estimating the distance. Was the door unlocked? Probably. If he could get over there, slam into the driver's seat quicker than these goons could get to him, he could lock the doors and get the fuck out before they had a chance to do him like Red.

Two of the goons picked Red up and positioned him on an angle, legs flopped to the sides, arms dangling. The third one, the one who'd jammed the pipe down the throat, stood eye level with the cocked head and bloody mouth. The body looked like a pig on a spit ready to be roasted. The creep grabbed the end of the pipe with two gangly hands and cradled his skeletal mouth in said hands, creating as airtight a seal as he could. He then blew, forcing air into the pipe. The way his eyes swelled up like little balloons attested to how deeply he blew, and how clogged the PVC pipe was.

Larry looked at the keys in his open palm. Located the big one. The car key. He shifted them so he had the key between thumb and forefinger, cringing at even the slightest metallic sound they made, but the goon blowing on the PVC was making such agonizing and sloppy wet sounds that none of them heard the keys jangle. Sweat beaded on his forehead as Larry watched intently, waiting for his moment.

It happened quickly. A dull, muffled sound issued from the corpse and the blockage was cleared. The bottom of the PVC shat out a tubular clump of bloody guts and bowels that hit the floor and softened into a pile of mush. The two goons holding the body let go of it and cheered in some animalistic fashion, as if they completely lost the ability to communicate like normal human beings. The one who blew through the PVC to unclog the tube fell backwards, smacking his head on the concrete floor so hard it cracked open.

Larry made a completely involuntary noise that was somewhere between a frightened little girl and a terrified special needs kid. He ran to the car, opened the door, and slammed the key into the ignition. The engine came to life, and he threw the thing into reverse without thinking about what he was doing. One final glance at the mayhem played out before his very eyes showed him two slobbering goons standing around two corpses. They stood still, just staring at Larry panicking in the car. Larry backed out of the loading dock and into the alley, not even checking for cars or people. He threw the car into gear and shot down the filthy street as if he didn't have a serious load of drugs in the trunk.

CHAPTER 8

Creating a fake Tinder profile was easy enough, but detailing and refining the profile to match a particular user was another thing altogether. On top of that, there was no telling how often this Larry guy used the Tinder app. His profile stated he was twenty-five (he looked at least thirty-seven in the pic), he was into classic rock, looking for someone who wanted some fun, but not a relationship. Classy guy. He was an equal opportunity womanizer. The profile actually said: "I like 'em thick or thin, tall or small, black or white, blonde or brunette... but no ugly chicks."

How the hell did her sister hook up with a scumbag like this? Everything about the guy raised red flags. Amber would have liked to see Erin's profile. Maybe she was also just looking for a good time. Amber couldn't understand why her sister had a Tinder account in the first place. She was a good-looking girl, even when she dyed her hair wild colors and wore torn up punk rock clothes. A lot of guys were into that look anyway. The kind of guys Amber figured her sister was interested in, the kind who were like her. The punks. But maybe things had changed. Amber knew what happened when people became absorbed into the drug culture. That was a look all its own. Drugs could wipe away an identity like rubbing down a dry erase board with a rag. Could be Erin was looking for some kind of drug hook up. When you're down and low on cash, a pretty girl could easily find a guy with the same monkey on his back more than willing to share his dope for some pussy. Amber loathed to think of her sister in such a way, but she was no fool and she refused to sugarcoat reality.

Amber put together a playful profile with plenty of overlap. Larry's profile had obvious drug euphemisms, so she did the same thing. It would be best to have him contact her; however, she would make the first move if necessary. If she played her cards right, Tinder would put them in contact as perfect matches. That would be great. A man this stupid and self-serving would be easy to nab. Question was, would this guy lead her to Erin?

Ready to finally get some sleep after an exhausting day of research and mind-numbing process of elimination, Amber showered and had just laid down in bed when she heard the commotion outside.

It was one in the morning on the mean streets of El Cajon. Amber hadn't gotten enough police training to feel comfortable leaving her room at that hour, so she got out of bed and looked out of the window to see what was going on.

A car pulled into the parking lot, but didn't choose a stall to park in. It sat idling in front of the motel. The passenger side door was open, and a man stood there exchanging words with someone else, presumably a motel resident. The resident was becoming irate, but Amber couldn't make out their words.

Others huddled around the car. They seemed to appear out of nowhere like roaches slipping out of nooks and crannies. The parking lot lights were bright, illuminating what appeared to be a group of zombies. They were all wasted away like the guy Amber had seen in the room below hers, faces deteriorated as if they had been splashed with corrosive acid. Some of them were hunched over, their appendages appearing a little bit elongated, as if their body structure was changing into grotesque versions of Slender Man.

The man who came out of the passenger's side of the car didn't look too rough for wear, not yet at least. Just rail thin and sunken in, the way Amber remembered tweakers to look. He continued exchanging words, and then things got physical. The motel resident pushed the passenger into the car. The passenger came after the man with a raised fist and that's when the gathering horde of street trash shifted in, surrounding him. At this point the driver stepped out of the car, waving his hands around, as if trying to get the attention of the street vermin, but they weren't having it. One guy lunged forward and palmed the passenger's face, his lanky fingers wrapping around the cranium impossibly like they were the arms of a starfish. He then slammed the passenger's head repeatedly against the frame of the car, just above the passenger's side door. *Thwack! Thwack! Thwack!*

Amber watched in horror, too petrified to do anything about it, and then she realized a call to the police was the only thing she *could* do. Were she to so much as step outside of her room she would be putting herself in grave danger. Better that they didn't even know she was there.

Grabbing her cell phone, Amber returned to the window to watch as she listened to the dial tone for 911 ring endlessly. Now the driver ran to the back of the car, shrugging off the onslaught of nasty street people. He popped the trunk and leapt back, away the converging group as they all went for whatever was inside. The man ditched his car, running across the parking lot but tripped in a pothole. He went down hard and some tweaker rode up on a BMX bike and rolled right over the guy's throat. His hands went to his neck as he scrambled around on the ground. He appeared to be gasping for breath.

The call to 911 rang and rang.

Amber watched as the TOAB abandoned his bike and walked back to the man who was squirming on the ground clutching his neck. The guy was probably suffering from a collapsed trachea. The tweaker slung his ratty backpack onto the ground and opened it up. He produced a long cylindrical item Amber thought looked an awful lot like a vibrator. She'd never been one to use vibrators, but she'd seen the Silver Bullet before at a bachelorette party or a friend's house or something. Maybe from back in her druggie days. The tweaker held the little silver tool like a knife and slammed it into the squirming man's head in a downward stabbing motion.

The call to 911 rang endlessly.

Finally, the tweaker managed to lodge the vibrator-looking object into the man's right eye. The tweaker then put the palm of his hand over the back of the Silver Bullet and pushed. Amber shuddered. The tweaker stood up and joined the group scavenging the trunk of the car. The driver lay there motionless with the end of the cylindrical object protruding from his bloody eye socket.

It was then Amber realized she'd been listening to the incessant ringing of her phone and help was not on the way. Help wasn't even answering. She'd heard 911 was often unresponsive in places like L.A. and New York City, but El Cajon? That was crazy.

She hung up and dialed 911 again. She averted her attention to the car. It was like a feeding frenzy, watching the tweaker freaks. They scrambled over one another like a disturbed ant pile, fiending for something in the trunk, and then Amber realized what this was all about. As they got their share, they scrambled away off into the shadows of their motel rooms. Others remained at the trunk of the car examining torn bags clouded with crystal meth residue. Black tongues emerged from sickening faces, licking the bags. Others clamored on the asphalt, picking tiny shards of meth out of the dirt like birds pecking for grubs.

Still the phone rang endlessly. The police were not going to come. Not tonight, for there must have been other emergencies *far more important* than double homicide.

The last of the scragglers searching for morsels of meth in the trunk and on the ground were enraged and turned on one another. Amber couldn't make out their words, but the commotion was even worse than when the car first pulled up. Something seemed to startle them, and they ran off, some on bikes and others on foot, moving like gazelles on long, spindly legs.

Amber hoped it was the police showing up, maybe someone else in the motel got through, but she stood there looking out the window for a good fifteen minutes before giving up hope.

The corpse lay there with that little silver thing protruding from its eye socket. Amber watched a bit longer. No one came by. No police, no other people staying in the motel. The body just lay there like it didn't matter.

Finally Amber said fuck it and decided to have a look at the thing. Normally she wouldn't have ventured out this late in this part of town, but the training she'd received at the academy had given her some confidence. There was a part of her that was fascinated with the opportunity of a quick investigation, even though she'd been there to witness exactly how the murder occurred.

Grabbing a hunting knife, she bought at the market earlier that day (she would have felt a lot more comfortable had she been in possession of a service weapon), Amber opened her door and crept outside stealthily, listening and watching for movement in and around the building. So far things were quiet. The fiends were satisfied with the loads of dope they pilfered from the car and were probably in their rooms loaded to the gills, stoned and happy.

Trepidation caused Amber to hesitate at the threshold of her room. What she'd seen was like a feeding frenzy witnessed only in the wilds of nature, something civilized human beings shouldn't have been subjected to. It was frightening to watch. Standing there on the upstairs landing of maybe the nastiest motel Amber had ever been in, she wondered whether her curiosities were getting the better of her. Was it really worth it for her to have a closer look at the body? What if the police arrived while she was crouched over the thing? What if they thought she killed the man?

It was the last thought which most threatened Amber to abandon her curiosities, but then a buzzing sound issuing from below causing her to abandon her fears, if only momentarily. She had her training and her knife if danger were to present itself.

Descending the stairs, the buzzing increased.

Bzzzzzzzzzzz.

No, it can't be, she thought.

Bzzzzzzzzzzz.

At the bottom of the stairs, she looked over her shoulder towards the front of the building. All the doors were closed. Yeah, they were definitely smoking their dope or shooting up.

Amber knelt next to the body, careful not to dip

her knees in the blood on the faded asphalt. The buzzing was coming from what indeed turned out to be a vibrator lodged in the man's eye socket. The freak who killed him made sure to turn the thing on. It was jammed in there pretty good too. She'd have thought the buzzing would have dislodged it.

"Hey!"

Amber's head darted up from the body at the sound of a voice. There was a deep instinctual fear that it was the cops. Even though she considered herself on their side these days, that old familiar feeling hit her like a frying pan to the face. It was deer-in-the-headlights sort of thing.

"I know you," the voice said.

Amber took a few steps away from the body, in the opposite direction of the voice. It seemed to be coming from a row of hedges across the parking lot.

"Don't let them see you out here," the voice said.

Squinting to see through the gaps in the hedge, Amber thought she recognized the voice. It was kind of like getting a whiff of some old perfume that brings back childhood memories. It was almost comforting in the current circumstance, and yet it was a weird reminder of where Amber came from before getting straight, deciding to become a police officer. The voice had to have been from *that* past, which meant it was probably some ex-boyfriend or drug buddy. Which also meant it was someone she didn't want anything to do with.

Heeding the man's advice, Amber retreated up the stairs, slipping into her room.

CHAPTER 9

Erin sat in the room for hours thinking about the strange man known as Dr. Scabs.

Hours. Days. Maybe just minutes. At this point, time was an illusion.

He'd given her a syringe. Along with her rule about knowing she'd gone overboard when she was picking imaginary bugs off her skin, Erin also had a strict rule about taking drugs intravenously. That was a major no-no. That was serious junkie shit. She figured once you started tapping the vein you were beholden to the drug. You weren't taking it for fun anymore. You were its bitch.

But Scabs was a doctor, right?

That's what he told her. He said he was a chemist, but a doctor, nonetheless. And doctors were not only very smart, but people to be trusted.

Even when their skin was covered in a thick layer of oozing scabs?

Erin stood and paced the room again. It was too much effort to sit still. She felt like a panther in a cage at the zoo. Pacing back and forth along the worn, threadbare carpet on the floor of what was once a break room? She was in an old strip mall, one on Second Street that had been abandoned for quite some time, though now it thrived with activity. It was all on the down-low, this activity, though Scabs was kind of secretive about what was really going on. He'd promised her that if she could stand the transformation (whatever that meant), then she would not only be filled in on everything, but become an important cog in his growing machine.

Whatever that meant.

He made the transformation sound majestic, though he gave no specific details on what it was. He said she would be a queen, lauded over and greatly respected in the underground. He told her she would be in a position of power. It was a lot to take in; after all, Erin was just a teenage girl who liked to have a good time. Yeah, she got heavy into the meth scene, and yeah, she was fairly certain it was eating her alive, but—

Goddamn she felt good. It felt as if she were floating on a sea of down feathers and freshly laundered comforters.

The stuff he gave her, it was unlike any meth she'd ever taken. For a moment there she thought he'd injected her with heroin, maybe he was just trying to get her addicted, but he assured her no, it wasn't heroin. It was something new.

"It's my special recipe," he said. "I only give this to those who have potential to become one of the queens, and I need a new queen. If you can handle it, you will oversee a part of the operation."

He was vague, and as soon as the drug hit her bloodstream, she found out two things: 1.) She understood why people used drugs intravenously. 2.) If Dr. Scabs could make her feel this good, she'd do anything for him.

He left after a few words of encouragement and vague mentions of the mysterious transformation. A becoming of sorts. A queen. A hag queen.

Whatever that was.

Erin didn't like the word *hag* being thrown around, not at first, but now she could feel something changing within her body, she was becoming used to the word. Hag. She said it aloud.

She let the word roll around her consciousness.

Hag queen. Vibrations bounced off the words like shimmering color in an oil slick.

Finally, Erin tried the door handle to get out and use a restroom or find somebody who could better explain what she was there for. She certainly didn't know. Her mind would trip out hard, like the peaks and valleys of an LSD high, and then she would be quite conscious of her current state in the room. That consciousness elicited fear. At least until the smooth, mercury waves of unbridled emotion made visions in her mind, grabbing her like the undertow in a rough sea and swept her into oblivion.

The door was locked, and though that would have normally alarmed her, she was quite all right being cooped up in the room. When she closed her eyes, she was on a limitless plane of consciousness. She was beginning to see things differently, to feel things differently. The room was small, but her consciousness was forever. That was something she had never considered before.

Eventually she laid down on the old couch (the only piece of furniture in the place), and closed her eyes, exploring the new vistas she was privy to. Her body twitched and spasmed like she were having a medical emergency, but Erin felt more at peace than she had in her entire life.

As she traveled the vast expanse of her mind, she allowed the things she once worried about to drop away like a snake shedding skin. There was no worry in this room, in this headspace. Her mother couldn't get to her here, couldn't bitch and complain about her appearance and her future. Her pig sister was gone to the dark side of law enforcement, and even if she came after Erin with a service revolver and a baton, she couldn't get her either. All of her loser ex-boyfriends couldn't get her here. The guys who would feed her booze and drugs, basically raping her unconscious body—*you know you wanted it*, they'd say—could fuck right off.

Erin convulsed as she lay on the couch, but the grin on her face was as wide as the muscles in her cheeks would allow. In her mind she was calm, unaware her body was going through some seriously fucked up shit on a dingy couch in an old strip mall in the middle of El Cajon, California. Halle-fuckin-luiah!

CHAPTER 10

——

Amber closed the door and promptly locked not only the handle, but the deadbolt as well as the little chain lock. She took a few steps back, just staring at the door as if the guy who was taunting her from the hedges would storm up the stairs and come a knockin'.

The image of the vibrator buzzing in the guy's eye socket was stuck in her head, just sort of looping over and over. She'd seen some shit when she was a druggie, but nothing even came close to that. And worse, the guy was still out there getting skull fucked by a sex toy and no one was coming to investigate.

What the actual fuck!

Shaking her head and feeling confident—well, sorta—that the hedge-dude wasn't coming after her, Amber turned, ready to drop onto the bed and attempt to sleep knowing there were a pair of dead junkies littering the pavement just outside, when she came face to face with a fucking monster of a man.

She screamed. A straight up bloodcurdling scream like the final girl in some 80's slasher film.

The man stood there in a black trench coat, his bare feet indicating he was some kind of flasher (*do people still do that?*). His face was hideously deformed, but not by birth, or the scars of an unfortunate accident. His deformation was like that of the man in the room below. His cheeks were shredded like someone had taken a rusty butter knife to them. His lips were crusted in dried blood, and his nose was gone. Just an open wound with two little holes and a glistening stream of loose snot that wheezed as he struggled to breathe. His pupils refused to dilate even in the brightness of the room. The whites of his eyes were the color of farm fresh egg yolks gone bad, etched with blown out purple capillaries.

"The shadow people told me you came in here," he said. "I thought I recognized you, but," he shook his head, "I don't know you."

"Get—"

"BUT!" he interjected. "I have something for you."

Oh fuck, this is where he opens the trench coat.

Thrusting the hunting knife out, Amber said, "Don't even fucking think about it. Just get the hell out of here."

The man grinned as if the knife was an offering. He grabbed the loose opening of his trench coat.

Oh shit. Here it comes.

But then Amber noticed something strange about the trench coat. It was large and hung loosely over his body, and yet there were parts appearing wet and clung to his skin. Had he pissed himself?

Amber shook her head. "No, no, no, you just get the fuck out of here." She back-stepped to the door, never taking her eyes off the freak.

He shook his head. "You want this, though. The shadow people told me you do."

Before she could get the locks undone, he yanked open his trench coat to reveal not only that he was in his birthday suit, but that his body was decorated with quite an array of cuts and gashes.

Amber clenched her teeth and squinted her eyes thinking she was about to see this guy's hard-on bobbing around a bush of pubic hair dotted with crabs, but this was so far out in left field that she was petrified in both fear and astonishment.

The man took a step forward and Amber swung the hunting knife. "You stay the *fuck* away!"

"B-but you don't get it, do you? My b-blood. It's, it's really good." He looked down at the red, oozing landscape of his chest and stomach. He'd cut right through tattoos, leaving them torn and fragmented. He stuck his finger in one of the particularly deep cuts and wiped off a thick coagulating chunk of blood. He looked at Amber with those sick eyes, curling his wretched maw into something like a grin, and put his finger into his mouth, his diseased tongue licking the blood clot. He shivered and moaned as the globule of blood loosened up with his acidic saliva. As he chewed the remaining clot it stuck to his teeth like he was eating bloody boogers.

"That's the good stuff," he said. "You just don't understand. It's in my blood, you see. You gotta lick me."

"You *gotta* fuck right off!"

He took another step forward. Amber brandished the knife threateningly, hoping it would stave him off enough for her to unlatch the locks on the door, which was challenging considering she wouldn't dare look away from this crazy man. She pivoted her body so her shoulder was against the door. One arm poised with the razor-sharp knife, she used her other hand to finagle the chain lock, which was insistent on not cooperating. In her frustration and panic, all she managed was to jiggle the thing around.

The man then raked his hand over his bloodied chest, digging his fingernails in the skin and over the previous wounds, tearing them open further. Fresh blood erupted, running down over his stomach, and gathering in the glistening nest of pubic hair. Clearly this wasn't a sexual thing, for he wasn't aroused. The blood gathering at his limp cock and balls dripped onto the carpet.

He held out his hands, dripping with fresh blood and dotted with dark, almost black clots that, absurdly in the moment, reminded Amber of menstruation blood. His mouth hung open so wide it was as if his jaw had been dislodged, displaying that he only had every other tooth. They stood there in his gums like old tombstones worse for wear and ready to fall. Pink saliva cascaded down his mouth from between his yellow teeth.

He moved forward again, this time with more purpose. It wasn't so much threatening as it was plain out creepy, like the guy sincerely wanted her to have a taste of his blood, and Amber wasn't going down like that.

She screamed, "Back off!" but he didn't so much as flinch.

He reached to stick a bloodied hand into her mouth and she forgot all of her training, because in this moment all she needed were survival instincts. Amber, white-knuckled the knife and lunged forward, avoiding a face full of bloody fingers as she lodged the blade into the man's throat. The sound that came out of her mouth when the knife went in was something primal between a yell of triumph and a shriek of fear.

It wasn't a clean stab. Amber learned that most stab wounds weren't as clean as were seen on TV and in the movies. The knife entered his throat and sort of severed his carotid artery right along with his windpipe. It was more like she slashed his throat than the intended stab.

The man was caught by surprise. He jerked back and stumbled, falling onto the floor so hard Amber thought he was going to collapse into the room below. He clutched at his neck with both hands and wheezed as blood spurted from his severed carotid artery, shooting across the room with less gusto from each dying heartbeat. His screams were muted, resulting in panicked gurgling as he choked to death on his own blood.

Amber dodged being spritzed with arterial flow squeezing through the man's fingers. She watched as he died. Blood gushed out of his neck like nothing she had ever seen. He lay still, dead, and the blood continued to wash down his naked body, saturating the trench coat and the carpet beneath.

It was bad enough Amber went AWOL from the police academy.

Now she was a murderer.

CHAPTER 11

———

Patricia Montgomery stood at her back door, staring through the glass at the sad state of her garden illuminated in the bright of a full moon. Only a week ago it had been flourishing. She expected a bounty of tomatoes, as usual, as well as green beans, bell peppers, snow peas, and plenty of zucchini. But, despite her efforts to water regularly, the plants were droopy and sad, a perfect reflection for the way Pat herself had been feeling since her daughter Erin went missing.

She'd feared Erin was showing similar signs like those she missed when her older daughter was the same age and taking drugs. Fortunately, Amber had a good head on her shoulder and realized she was heading down a dangerous path. It pleased Pat to no end when Amber declared she was going to join the police academy. Really, she was frightened by the line of work Amber chose, but it was noble work, and it would keep her clean.

Erin, on the other hand, had always been mischievous, even as a little girl. Always sneaking cookies into her room at night after brushing her teeth, changing grades on her report card (everything went computerized and really foiled her poor attempts), sneaking out at night. Erin was a handful, and though Pat shouldn't have been surprised when Erin ran away, she couldn't help but feel not only disappointed, but sad and lost.

At least had Amber been there, she would have had someone to talk to about Erin. The police were no help. Even Pat's friends from church dismissed Erin's behavior as typical for a teenager. *She'll be back*, they'd say, trying to be comforting. Seemed like they always managed to bring the conversation back to them, and how their son or daughter ran away one time, or how they knew someone whose daughter ran away. They didn't care. No one cared.

They all let Pat wilt away just like her garden.

She expected to feel empty nest syndrome, but not like this. She was proud of Amber for not only pursuing her dreams, but winning the battle against her demons. That was strictly a figure of speech, though some of the ladies at church believed things like sex, drugs and rock 'n' roll were actually demon influence warping the minds of the youth. Pat was deep into her religion, but she wasn't crazy. She didn't believe in literal demons walking the earth or communicating to people through music or illicit substances. Nancy, Jeanie, and Sue could believe all the mumbo jumbo they wanted.

Had Erin gone off to college after high school, Pat would have been heartbroken only because both of her children were gone, but that would have been temporary, and it never would have overshadowed the pride she would have felt having raised two outstanding citizens.

Erin running off filled Pat with self-loathing and sorrow. She kept thinking about their last interactions, which weren't anything out of the ordinary. Erin became so distant that Pat hardly even knew the girl anymore. But those thoughts nagged at Pat's mind, taunting her. What could she have done differently? Could she have been there more for Erin?

Did I do something wrong?

She wanted to call Amber, but it was too late. Pat wasn't entirely sure how the police academy worked, but she figured it was something like boot camp, not that she really knew how that worked either. In her mind she saw Amber sleeping in a big room of cots with other cadets. Lights out at a certain time. Each meal at a certain time. Phone calls were probably only allowed at a certain time. Like the other day when Amber called and Pat told her about Erin disappearing. Amber seemed concerned on the phone, but what could she do being way up state?

Pat was on her own, and she just didn't know what to do. What she saw on the news tonight was frightening. The crime rates in all of San Diego County seemed to be jumping exponentially, and here her daughter was lost in the mix somewhere.

Probably a statistic.

Pat tried not to think like that, but it didn't work. She thought like that all night long. One thing about Erin was the girl always had a rebellious side, even more so than her older sister. Pat noticed with other families that the older siblings always seemed to be the rebels, and the younger siblings often calmed down, learning from the mistakes of their older brothers and sisters, but not in this case. Erin seemed to look at the stupid things Amber did when she was a reckless teenager and considered them a challenge. If Amber got caught sneaking out of the house when she was sixteen, Erin did it when she was fourteen. If Amber got expelled from school at seventeen, Erin beat her by two years.

Until Pat found the drug paraphernalia in Erin's room just the other day, she had no idea her youngest was using. That was one of those things Erin hadn't seemed to follow in her sister's footsteps, though Pat should have suspected. She felt like a foolish idiot for not being more attentive. It might have been the reason for Erin's recent mood swings. Pat chalked it up to *teenagedom*, but she was wrong.

Pat had never been afraid of going out, but what she saw on the news had her double and triple checking the locks on the doors. It wasn't just petty crimes that had gone up, but violent crimes as well. Murder, rape, theft, arson. So much crime that the police department was having a hard time keeping up.

Pat closed the blinds on her patio doors, suddenly fearful someone could be out there watching her, ready to invade her house. She didn't live in the best neighborhood, but it wasn't a bad place to live either. El Cajon had been developing a bit of bad reputation over the years, but she was more on the outskirts. It was an old neighborhood, built in the late forties when construction in the area was booming after the war. Pat and Jake bought the house years ago after the original owners sold it to live their golden years in a retirement community. These days, the neighborhood consisted of the elderly or renters. Pat figured you could pretty much tell who was renting by the state of their front yard. Renters didn't take care of their houses like homeowners did. Also, rental properties brought in the riffraff. At least that's what she thought.

After checking the locks once again (as well as a few windows that were open earlier in the day), she sat on the couch with a blanket for comfort more than warmth. The TV was on, as it always was, but just for background, something to banish the silence weighing on her mind, driving her mad. She sat there and thought about everyone in her life who had walked out on her, for better or worse. First was her husband. Jake worked hard, was active in their church, didn't drink or smoke. He was reserved, but Pat always told people *that's just Jake*. It took time for him to warm up to folks, but when he did, he would. Jake wouldn't give anyone the shirt off his back or even help a friend move, but he was okay to be around. He was decent company.

Then one day he up and left. Simple as that. Left for work in the morning and didn't come back. The girls were devastated. Pat was inconsolable for days, mostly because it was so sudden and without reason. He left no note, no messages, nothing. A suitcase was missing, along with some clothes and a few random items including his gun and a bible that had been in his family for decades.

Church was the one place where Pat found comfort and support, outside of her two daughters. She'd always been a God-fearing woman, but after Jake left she dedicated herself to Christ, even if both her daughters seemed to have lost their religion that devastating day.

Next to leave was her mother, but that was to be expected with age and the cancer. God took another good one for his flock and Pat couldn't blame him for it. She wished she had more time with Mom, but it wasn't in God's plan, and so she just accepted it.

Next Amber left for the police academy. Pat couldn't be prouder. That girl had been through a lot and to see her come out the other end was a blessing. The thought of Amber having to go out in a uniform with the quickly worsening state of the county was terrifying.

And now it was Erin to leave in the same manner the girl's father did. Here today, gone tomorrow. No note. No warning. Nothing. There weren't clear signs of her walking out like a missing suitcase, so Pat didn't completely consider Erin's disappearance a betrayal like her father. The poor girl could have been kidnapped or murdered or something. Pat watched enough true crime shows on TV to know how common those sorts of crimes were.

She laid on the couch, pulling the blanket tightly to her body. She closed her eyes, but there were so many worries dancing in her mind that sleep did not come easy. She decided she would call Amber in the morning.

CHAPTER 12

Amber stood there staring down at the corpse for several minutes before deciding to call the police.

They didn't answer.

The line was busy this time.

What the fuck am I going to do?

A peek through the blinds revealed to her that the other bodies were still outside on the pavement. No flashing blue and red lights. A stray dog was gnawing on one of them, whipping its head back and forth like dogs do when playing with a sock with a knot tied in it, or when they're trying to rip flesh off of some poor sod's fucking face. Amber cringed.

She couldn't understand why there was no police presence. Where the hell were they? Wasn't someone working the front desk in the lobby? Why haven't they called the cops?

Turning from the window, she caught sight of the dead man on the floor and shuddered. It was hard to believe she'd done that to him, but what else could she do? That's why she called the police because this was an act of self-defense. The problem, the reason it took her so long to make the call she should have made seconds after the man bled out onto the carpet, was that once the police arrived and took down her name and statement, they would find out that she'd gone AWOL from the academy. That would surely get her in hot water, whether they believed she'd acted in self-defense or not.

Now she didn't know what to do, so she figured a call to the lobby was in order. Maybe the best way to get things rolling was to alert the desk clerk about the dead bodies outside.

The phone on the scarred stationary desk was an ugly throwback to the eighties. It had once been pink, now coated in so much grime it looked like it was salvaged from the depths of a landfill and planted there in the motel room where it fit nicely considering how clean the place was. On the phone were two numbers written on little pieces of paper behind a clear plastic shield that somehow wasn't too smudged or burnt to see through (there were burn marks from cigarettes all over the stationary desk, mostly on the edges where people set their cigarettes down rather than using an ashtray). One number was 911 (as if anyone would have trouble remembering that one), and the other was for the front desk. Amber used her cell phone to make the call.

The desk clerk answered after three rings. "Midtown Motel."

It was a man with a faint Indian accent. He sounded either irritated or flustered, it was hard to tell which. Maybe a combination of the two.

"Uh, uh..." Amber found herself unable to articulate her concerns. Just how do you report two men had been murdered in front of the place about an hour ago?

"For fuck's sake!" the desk clerk said. Clearly, he was irritated, not flustered. "Spit it out, will you."

"I'm staying at the motel, and I saw two people get murdered outside. About an hour ago."

"Yeah, yeah, I know. I saw 'em. What do you want me to do about it?"

Amber wrinkled her brow. "What do you mean?

Have the police been called? I couldn't get through to them."

"Yeah, no shit. No one can. Two nights ago, someone was murdered out there right before my eyes by a couple of ugly lookin' junkie types. I called the cops *while it was happening*, and you know what? Nothing. Phone just rang and rang until finally I called, and it was busy, if you can believe that shit."

"Well..." Amber fully intended on telling the desk clerk about the dead man in her room. It was self-defense and all.

"Well, nothing. You sound too straight to be staying at this place. If I were you, I'd lock the door and stay in until sunrise, then get the fuck out of here. This isn't a place for regular people. You know what? I have the fucking lobby doors locked. That's how bad it is. I won't open them for anything at this point. I don't even know why they have me come in at night anymore. It's just too goddamned dangerous out there at night." The desk clerk sighed. "I don't get paid enough for this shit." That last comment was more to himself than to Amber.

"Okay, okay." Amber didn't know what to say. "I didn't know things were *that* bad."

"You didn't know?" She could hear a grin on the man's face. "You didn't *know*? Where in sweet fuck have you been? This town's been going to shit for a while now." He chuckled, and then said, "Like I said, you should get out in the morning. If you're passing through, you picked a hell of a place to stay. Honestly, this is probably my last night here. I'd leave now, but I don't want to end up like the guys outside. Sorry, but I can't do anything for you."

He hung up on her.

Amber sat there on the edge of the bed thinking about everything that happened in the last twenty-four hours, and the state of El Cajon. It was bad before she left for the academy, but that was only a month ago. How had it gotten so much worse? Things can change around a person or even a neighborhood, sometimes so slowly at first that no one really notices how bad things are getting. How different. But it seems that in the past few weeks El Cajon has gone down the shitter, and fast. How many other motels were out there facing the same issues with extreme violence, night after night, and how many of them have desk clerks who will be abandoning their positions for the sake of safety?

Shit was about the get real.

Amber wrinkled her nose on the scent of blood in the air. She'd heard that people tended to release their bladder and bowels when they were deceased. This guy didn't smell like shit, so she was thankful for small favors. He pissed himself though. It was unhealthily yellow, which made it visible on his pale thighs.

The desk clerk said not to go outside, but Amber would be damned if she was going to sit here with a fucking corpse in her motel room, even if she did have plans to leave in the morning.

The guy was skinny. Not just that, he was malnourished, his bones a phantom outline beneath his pale, yellowish flesh. Amber figured he was 110 soaking wet. Probably been hooked on meth or heroin or both for so long he'd just wilted away to nothing but a sickly shell of his former self. He lacked muscle tone. Amber wouldn't have been surprised to find out his bone density was down, as well. He had the body of an elderly man, but was clearly in his thirties or forties.

Amber was smart enough to see where substance abuse would lead her. She saw the writing on the wall and learn from the mistakes of her friends. This was the outcome. At the time she'd thought her friends had it going on. They'd gotten so skinny it was amazing, but along with it they'd lost their tits and ass and eventually their goddamned teeth. Not to mention the acne and scratching resulting in pockmarks and scars. Hanging around women who picked at their faces and looked like such messes was one of the reasons Amber decided to straighten up.

And here she was in a druggie motel with a dead man all bled out onto the carpet and cooling into rigor mortis. No help from the cops. No help from the front desk. She was on her own.

The thought of going to sleep with the guy in there freaked her out. It was ridiculous, but she couldn't help imagining waking up and finding the corpse standing over her bed, just staring down at her like a zombie. Those were completely irrational thoughts, but how often did Amber have a dead guy in her presence?

Shivers scaled Amber's legs and up her back to her arms.

No, she wasn't going to stay there with a dead man.

After a deep sigh and vigorously rubbing her temples as if it would somehow wipe away the headache that seeped in somewhere between examining the vibrator in a dead man's eye socket and killing a man in her motel room, Amber knelt and grabbed the naked corpse's feet. She grunted and pulled, relieved when his tiny frame was indeed as light as she'd anticipated.

Swinging him around, she dragged the man backwards toward the door. Light or not, it was a hell of an effort, and the strain did no favors for her increasing headache. He slid off the thickening blood pool like a Slip 'n' Slide, after which his sticky back dragged on the tight-napped carpet. Crouched down, Amber took in a deep breath and heaved backwards with all her might as she exhaled. She made it to the door in four hefty pulls of his spindly legs.

She opened the door and had a look outside. Nothing new. The dog continued to nibble on vibrator-face, unaffected by Amber's presence on the second floor landing. It was somewhere around two or three in the morning, which meant nothing in a place like this. Those freaks who'd attacked and killed the men below were awake in their rooms, no doubt, minds spinning like tops. Amber would have to make this quick and get back into her room, hopefully unseen, though she really didn't care what a bunch of crazed drug fiends saw. They all had closets loaded with skeletons. And motel rooms loaded with dope. They didn't want police here.

Pulling the corpse's legs, she removed half the body from the room before slamming into the railing rump first. The iron railing wailed metallically, the shifty movement of the thing startling Amber, causing her to flinch as if it would collapse and she'd take a fall to the asphalt below, joining the dead and wait for a cop, cleanup crew or maybe a hungry dog.

The naked man's legs and lower torso were out of the room, but his chest, arms and head were still inside. She couldn't pull him straight back with the iron railing in the way.

She dropped his feet and they both slipped between the iron rungs, hanging over the ledge of the second story walkway. Amber looked down at the man and tilted her head, then nodded when an idea struck her. She stepped over him into the room, careful not to get his blood on her, but the stuff was everywhere. It was impossible to avoid, and it smelled terrible. The coppery odor was heavy in the room and was changing in quality, threatening her gag reflex. Once she managed to get him the fuck out of there, she was going to have to figure out a way to cover the sticky puddle up.

Goddamn this is wrong. This is so fucking wrong.

From the inside, Amber fumbled around trying to kneel behind the man and not dip her knees in the bloody trail, but it proved impossible. One knee went right into the blood and she could feel the wetness seep through to her skin. Fortunately, she had a change of clothes in her duffel from the academy, but the feeling of some rando's blood on her skin made her cringe. She sat back, sitting on the heels of her feet, shoulders slumped.

Warm city-street-stinking air blew in taking Amber from her pity party, reminding her she needed to be quick before someone else in the building saw her open door, taking that as an invitation. They wouldn't care about the body. They were vermin. You left an opening exposed and they snuck in, just like this drink-my-blood motherfucker had.

And look what it got you, asshole!

Considering her knee was saturated in his blood, Amber gave up on cleanliness, figuring she would take a scorching hot shower once this was all over with. The AIDS test would have to wait until all this business investigating her sister's disappearance was over. Planting her hand firmly in the man's shoulders (trying not to touch his self-inflicted wounds), she pushed him as hard as she could. At first, he wouldn't budge, as if the blood on his back had dried to the carpet like glue. Once he gave, his body slid over the threshold and onto the concrete landing, which must have given his back quite a raspberry, not that he would mind. His chicken legs slid through until his flaccid little penis slammed into an iron spindle. Amber cringed watching his junk take an iron railing that way. Dead or not, it looked painful.

Now his head was on the threshold and Amber was in no mood to pussyfoot around with her decisions on how to get the bastard out of there. She was covered in his blood, all thick and sticky and chunky. She grabbed the back of his head and hefted it up, pushing to the side to get the thing out of the room. The back of his head slid down the stucco, contorting his body in a weird way. Amber stepped over him and stood above his head on the landing. She grabbed his arms and yanked, but he was all twisted up in the iron railing, his legs catching and not allowing his body to be pulled away from the door. Leaving him out there like that would be an invitation to the crime scene.

Then again, there was a bloody trail leading right into her room, and there was no way she would be washing that away.

Fuck it.

Just getting the body out was good enough for now. She wouldn't be staying there any longer than she had to. Amber reminded herself it was all done in self-defense, though she figured moving the body outside like that broke a law or two.

She stripped the comforter off the bed and draped it over the massive bloodstain where the guy bled out onto the carpet. She made no attempt in cleaning it up, just wanted to cover the area so she didn't go traipsing around in it in the middle of the night. She didn't want to be a total mess when they arrested her later.

After a shower hot enough to melt skin off—*at least I'd fit in with the freaks around here*—Amber crawled into bed and closed her eyes. Despite everything that happened in the past few hours, she was exhausted. Her mind ran laps, playing and replaying the tragic events of murdering the naked man and dragging his body out of the room. The more she thought on it, the more she convinced herself it was strictly self-defense. Moving the body? Well, that was another story, but what was a girl to do? If the police weren't coming, she had to do something.

Fully expecting to be woken up by loud pounding on the door at any moment through the rest of the night, somehow Amber drifted off to sleep.

CHAPTER 13

Dr. Scabs sat in a cheap wooden chair behind an office desk that had been left behind in one of the suites in the strip mall he commandeered several months ago. Word around the campfire was that the strip mall was scheduled to be demolished in a year or so to begin construction on a more modern strip mall. Scabs figured if he moved into the place on the sly no one would notice, especially with crime skyrocketing. The police didn't have time to investigate what they would assume to be squatters when lunatics were out raping and murdering random people at unprecedented levels.

Scabs heard on the news that cops were already applying in different districts. The mayor of El Cajon was working on an order to prohibit police from transferring, at least for a limited time, though that seemed to be caught in red tape. Some cops were just resigning or even quitting. One of them was on the news. Said he took up the badge to serve and protect, but the state of El Cajon was so bad he felt like he'd been thrown into downtown Detroit or something.

Scabs didn't want world domination or anything like that, but he was pleased to see how his influence on this microcosm of society was playing out. There was talk about sending the National Guard, but that was all right wing chest puffing, immediately depressed, pushed down by the left who insisted it was a sign of political dominance. El Cajon was a minority community, for the most part, and that would be regarded as poorly as Regan sending tanks into the streets of Los Angeles to deal with the crack epidemic in the eighties.

Just so long as the political left and right were bickering at one another, Scabs had nothing to worry about. His army grew larger every minute, with every line snorted for the first time, every inhale of the latest batch of super meth, every hot needle injection into the arm of an unsuspecting soul who'd gotten a taste.

That was the key. Get them all to take the stuff intravenously.

Snaggle walked into the room without knocking. Scabs leaned back in his chair (as much as he could in a cheapo wooden Ikea chair). His eyes deepened, glistening in a face of scabbed-over flesh.

Snaggle shifted around in rapid movements indicative of how fast his drug-fueled mind was spinning. Scabs had been thinking about eliminating him. He was making mistakes and fighting the natural law of the super meth. His mind was becoming putty, and though that made him easy to manipulate, it also turned him into a clumsy fucking idiot. He should be out there with the other night stalkers, roaming the streets of El Cajon, causing mayhem. If the police got him, so be it. They'd have to take him down with a bullet, but there were plenty more where Snaggle came from.

"Are you with me, Snaggle?" Scabs said. He absentmindedly picked at a scab on her ear. When he didn't get a response, Scabs snapped his fingers (something he was able to do effortlessly since the palms of his hands and bottoms of his fingers were areas devoid of scabbed flesh).

Snaggle looked up, breathing heavily through

shreds of flesh that used to be lips, dangling from his mouth like thick little flesh dreads. His head changed, molting into something alien. The ears were gone, leaving holes on either side with wild hairs sprouting like blades of wilted grass. His eyes were lighter in color, an interesting development in the mutation Dr. Scabs was only recently aware of. It was as if they were getting cataract, but why? Scabs knew once the change happened their senses became excited. Particularly their sense of hearing. But why would their eyes go cataract?

The paranoia was often a side effect of illicit drug use stifled, which was probably why there was so much crime. When the tweaker creatures got going, they couldn't be stopped, and they just didn't give a fuck about anything. With a complete loss of empathy and morals, basic humanity, the tweaker creature was truly a beast.

"I'm here," Snaggle said. "All, uh, ears." Words hissed out of his mouth through tendrils of shredded flesh-lips. The man's breath was rank old onions and burning plastic.

Scabs picked at his ear again. "We've got another hag. She needs a house. Do we have anywhere ready to take her? A house we can take over without arousing too much suspicion. I imagine it won't be too hard. I've seen the news." Scabs painfully smiled. "Things are coming along nicely."

Snaggle's black tongue ran over his toothless maw incessantly, flicking the fleshy tendrils dangling there. "Uh, well, nothing right now. We could always just take someone's house. That shouldn't be a problem. People are hunkering down though. That's what I heard."

Scabs nodded. "Yeah, I would imagine so." He pulled a flake of scab off his ear. He eyed the ornery bastard that had been itching him so, and then placed it on his tongue like a tab of acid, relishing the tiny morsel.

The swollen flesh around Snaggle's eyes danced and cringed, as if the act of chewing one's scabs was far more grotesque than scratching at his face until his features shredded away. To each their own.

"I can only control those of you on the streets so much. I knew once this stuff got out to the masses it would be a shit show." Scabs shook his head. "That's okay. It will be a while before they send the National Guard, and by then the National Guard won't be able to do anything." He leaned in, elbows on his desk, and smiled, cracking dark scabs forming around his mouth. A couple drops of blood seeped from the crevices. "How are you, ole Snaggletooth? How are you feeling?"

Snaggle's eyes were wild. "I'm good, I guess. I've been, uh, I've been going through some shit. Changes. Seeing the shadow people a lot more."

Scabs feigned a look of surprise. "You don't say. Shadow people, huh?"

"Yeah. They kind of come out of the shadows, where they hide. They talk to me. Tell me to do things. I used to be scared of them, but they're my friends.

"Interesting. Anything else?"

"Um, well, you see, my face has felt a little weird. I think it's all *swoled* up. But I feel good. Really I do. I feel the best. It's just when I look at myself in the mirror, I'm not me."

Scabs tapped his head with a finger several times. "How about up here? You feeling okay up in the ole noggin? Outside of seeing shadow people."

To this Snaggle grinned, which an awful thing to see, considering the state of his mouth. "Oh yeah, I feel like a million fucking dollars up here. I feel like I can do anything I want and no one can stop me."

Scabs nodded. "That's right. That's good. But what do you want out of life?"

Snaggle soured for a moment, then the sickening grin resurfaced. "I just want to feel everything. I want to... I want to become *experience*. I want to live with the shadow people."

Scabs nodded slightly. "Interesting." He took a deep breath and leaned back in his chair. Started picking at a scab on his arm. "So, what about the new hag. I can't have her here. It's too risky. This is more of a hub of operations. I need the hags in unsuspecting houses. This place, I'm sure it's being surveyed, or at least *was* being surveyed. The hag houses, however, blend in well with everyone else. Let's keep it that way.

Snaggle ran his dirty hands over the swollen flash of his head.

Scabs narrowed his eyes. "Is there a problem? Do I need to find someone else who can help me?"

Snaggle was quick to answer. "No, oh no no no. I-I can do it. No problem. I'll find a place."

"I want her moved there within twenty-four hours. That gives us a total of four hag houses. That's good." Scabs nodded. "Yeah, that's real good. That will bump up production. At this rate I'll have double the hag houses in the next few months. Then I branch out."

Sweat rippled across Snaggle's distorted flesh, almost as if he had a thin layer of candle wax coating his skin that was melting. He was all jittery and nervous.

"What the hell is the problem?" Scabs asked, beginning to lose his cool.

Snaggle licked his lips even more frantically. His words were but a strained whisper. "I need a taste."

"A tas—" Scabs squinted, and then he got it. "Oh! You need some stuff."

Snaggle nodded emphatically.

"For fuck's sake, guy." Scabs opened the drawer in his desk and pulled out a freezer sized Ziploc bag of ugly looking crystal meth and tossed it on the desk.

Snaggletooth started salivating like Pavlov's freak. It was uncontrollable. His mouth rained saliva like a dog confronted with a beef stick.

Scabs shook his head. "Goddamn you're a sorry fuck. But you're my sorry fuck." He opened the bag and pulled out a couple of shards the size of a pencil broken in half. He handed them over, quickly wiping his hands of the sticky substance they were coated with.

"Goddamn that's nasty," Scabs said.

Snaggle shook his head. "No way, that's fresh."

"Indeed. Now you can shoot it, kiester it, smoke it, whatever you fucking want to do with it. Just do it somewhere else. Get the fuck out of here. And remember to get a house lined up. That's priority *numero uno*, got it?"

Snaggle nodded and quickly fled the office.

Scabs sighed deeply. "Poor fuck won't last much longer. Once he's lost his mind, he's only good enough for the street army." He picked the scab off his arm, wincing as it was freed from his body. He sucked air in through his clenched teeth. Examining the scab, he became soothed, forgetting the minor irritation of removing it. It was a large one, the size and shape of a cockroach. He put the scab in his mouth, licking the wet underside of the thing, then used his teeth to scrape off the soft, sticky goo. After swishing his tongue around in a circular motion to lick the thick gooey part of the scab off his front teeth, he chewed the crusty part, momentarily satisfying himself.

I know a house we can use.

Scab's eyes popped open as he sat straight in the chair. He smiled, ignoring the pain as the scabs around his frown lines widened.

CHAPTER 14

Larry and Pizzo drove down Broadway on their way to scout the new hag house. Larry drove. He'd always been a bit of a control freak, though he'd also worked for very controlling people. Unable to get his shit together, he took odd jobs selling dope, robbing, and roughing people up, always hoping to stumble upon a big score allowing him to retire from this life of crime and live like a regular schmo.

Larry had known Pizzo for a few years now. They hung in the same groups, at the same houses. Really it was their taste for speed that was the common bond. Pizzo was trying to quit, but look at the guy now. He was a mess.

At a stoplight, Larry looked over at Pizzo. "You look like shit, bro. Like seriously. You're not taking that fuckin' new crazy crack shit everyone's on, are you?"

Pizzo looked over at Larry, one eye almost completely closed, seeping yellowy juice. The other eye was open, but alive with nasty busted capillaries, like he'd been violently vomiting for hours on end, which he probably had.

Larry shook his head. "You did try it, didn't you? Just the other day you told me you wouldn't try that new shit. What happened? You know that's what's making people get so fuckin' crazy." Larry shook his head and accelerated now that the light turned green.

Pizzo didn't say a word.

Larry said, "I saw a guy the other night who

wasn't a guy no more. Know what I'm saying? I mean, not like the guy was a tranny or something. No, not that. Like he mutated or something. I've seen a bunch of guys like that, but this one was something else, man. Like seriously, he was all fucked up. Changed." Larry stuck a cigarette in his mouth and lit it. "Fuck, man. I don't know. It's that crazy meth. Seriously, man. That shit is fuckin' turning people into..." he shook his head, flicked his ash and took another drag. "I don't know what, but it's bad. What's worse?" Larry looked at Pizzo, eyebrows raised as if Pizzo was going to take a shot at telling him what was worse. "What's worse is that you can't find good ole regular ice anymore." Larry laughed. "Can you believe that, man? What a fucked up world."

They turned down Mollison Avenue and drove past Pepper into a quiet little neighborhood at the base of Rattlesnake Mountain. Houses built in the fifties dotted the street on both sides. What once were cookie cutter tract homes were now modified to create the illusion they were all custom built, all except for a few that still had outdated features, probably owned by the old people who bought them when they were young.

"It's up in here," Larry said.

Pizzo nodded. "Quiet neighborhood." He grunted, then cleared something phlegmy from his throat and hacked it onto the floorboard.

"The fuck you doing, man!"

Pizzo glared with his one open eye, hacked up again and hocked a fat globule of red, sticky goo on the floorboard. "What the fuck are you gonna do about it?"

Larry pulled the car up to the curb in front of an old house with a slightly unkempt yard. He put the car in park and left the engine running. Leveling his gaze at Pizzo, he said, "Who the fuck do you think you are coming in here and hacking up in my fucking car? Huh?"

"It don't matter."

"The hell it doesn't! Look, man, I might be out here hustling and slinging dope 'n' shit, but I'm not going to throw my life away for that goddamned super crank everybody's losing their fucking minds over, okay. You've obviously been dipping into your supply. That's what they want. They want you hooked. Me, I've been cutting my supply and pocketing half the money. They don't want to pay us shit to sell this stuff because they think we'll get hooked and be happy pinching off the stuff we're selling. They got these houses around town we can stay in. Well fuck that. I don't want to stay in one of these hag houses anyway. It's fuckin' nasty. I'm making bank off cutting the stuff and selling twice as much, and I'm gonna keep it that way until I have enough money to get the fuck out of here before this whole town implodes."

While Larry was on his rant, Pizzo pulled out his kit, suddenly not giving a shit his old buddy knew how deeply invested in the super meth he was. He put a few little shards in a bent spoon, pulled out a lighter, and swirled a flame beneath to melt the stuff down.

"You never took shit into your veins before, man," Larry said. His voice dropped, showing hints of concern. "The fuck happened to you?"

Pizzo pulled out what was clearly an old, used needle and sucked up the liquid meth. He looked Larry in the eye and said, "Scabs ain't gonna be happy when he finds out you ain't doin' this shit. This is kind of the deal. You gotta go in all the way, dude."

Larry shook his head. "No, not me. Fuck that.

Besides, how the fuck is Dr. Scabs gonna find out?"

After tying off his arm with a cut of electrical cord from a stereo or TV or something, he jabbed the needle into his vein, depressed the plunger, and his body went rigid for a moment. He took in a deep inhale and held it there, then let it out saying, "He'll find out when I tell him," as he exhaled.

The needle dangled from his arm. It had dried blood on it from previous usage. Somebody's blood.

Larry shook his head. "Pull that fucking needle out of your arm, Nikki Sixx. Jesus Christ, man."

Pizzo's skin flushed. The eyelid that was sealed shut cracked open, but the eye concealed within was all wrong. It looked alien. Larry couldn't stand to look at the thing without cringing. Not only that, but Pizzo's skin changed right before Larry's watchful eyes. It seemed to *stretch*.

Pizzo took more deep breaths. He scratched at his face. His fingernails had grown long, and the flesh had little give, tearing off in tiny pieces. There was little blood, almost as if he were going through some kind of psycho-natural process of shedding his skin. Larry was transfixed for a moment, just taking it all in and wondering how much of this shit he could handle before he left town.

"Bugs?" Larry asked.

Pizzo shook his head. "Nirvana."

Larry shuddered. "Look, you ready for this? I don't know what to expect inside. Word is it's just a middle-aged woman, but who knows."

"Oh, I'm good and ready now. I've got fire in my veins."

Larry nodded. "I bet you do." He shook his head, second and third guessing his life decisions. Maybe a jail cell would be better than cavorting around with these super meth freaks.

His fucking head is misshapen!

Fuck it. Just get this over with.

"Ready?" Larry said.

Pizzo raised a finger as if to say, "just a moment". He made obnoxious noises as he ran his tongue across the remaining teeth in his closed mouth. Finally, he made a sound of eureka and spit out a tooth that ricocheted off the dashboard.

Larry cringed. "Fucking hell, man. You hack up lung butter on my floorboards and now you're spitting out your goddamned teeth. What's next?"

Pizzo opened his maw to reveal that he only had a few teeth left, nestled in red, inflamed gums. His tongue was purple, like a venomous snake lying in wait within the swollen cave of his rancid meth-mouth.

Shaking his head, Larry opened the door and got out of the car. The air outside tasted fresh and was welcoming compared to the insanity he'd just witnessed. As they took the walkway up to the house, Larry decided Pizzo wasn't going to make it out alive.

CHAPTER 15

—·—

Was it traveling the astral plane? Was it telepathy? A dream?

Erin had no idea, but she knew one thing. Whatever it was, she liked it.

But the comedown was awful. She lay on the couch in the room somewhere within the old strip mall, alone and shaking. She'd vomited several times on the floor and was now at the stage of dry heaving. It was a dope-sickness she'd never experienced before. And there was no one there to help her.

Her muscles tightened up as if they were clenching her bones. Her head ached like it were on an anvil under a blacksmith's hammer. Nausea was a constant; therefore, Erin closed her eyes to avoid feeling as if she were swirling in a maelstrom.

When she was twelve years old and first drank liquor, she and her best friend Katy got so hammered they got the spins and puked their guts out in the field out behind her grandmother's house, at the bottom of Rattlesnake Mountain. They puked and laid out there in the grass for hours until they felt somewhat normal. Erin swore she would never drink again. She would never do anything that would cause her to feel that way.

The following weekend they found someone to buy them a couple of forty-ounce bottles of Mickey's and did it all over again, assuming beer would be a better alternative to the hard liquor they'd pilfered from her grandmother's cabinet. The girls found the beers to be far more relaxing, and it looked cool to drink them out of paper bags like a couple of winos outside of the liquor store.

Back in those days, Erin idolized her sister Amber, before she went pig and joined the police academy. Just the thought of her own flesh and blood being a cop disgusted her. Amber had been so cool. She had cool friends. She smoked weed, drank and listened to cool music. What the hell happened to her?

Erin writhed on the couch, her guts clenching like she was in the midst of a terrible case of food poisoning. The way she felt, she could just shit her pants right there and not give a good goddamn. She was locked in there with no bathroom access. If someone didn't come in soon there was going to be a nasty accident.

Erin took deep breaths and moaned. She tended to have bad periods that over-the-counter painkillers could hardly quell. This comedown was worse. Thoughts about never using again teetered in her mind. But that feeling. The weightlessness. The floating through space and time. It was amazing. If only she could get there again.

Amber had come to Erin before she joined the academy. She expressed concern for her younger sister, but Erin laughed it off, to which Amber shook her head and said, "You're just like me. Maybe one day you'll get it."

That was one of the most depressing conversations of Erin's life. She immediately called a friend and they scored a joint dipped in hash oil, smoked it up on Rattlesnake Mountain, and that's when Erin wrote her pig sister off. She hardly spoke a word to Amber in the weeks that followed as Amber prepared to leave. In fact, Erin started hanging out with some seriously sketchy people in that time. The types she thought her sister would have liked before she joined the Dark Side. They were nothing but nice to Erin. Introduced her to LSD, oxys, crack, even shirm, which was a joint dipped in formaldehyde (the guy who smoked it with her said he snuck into the autopsy room at his father's funeral home and dipped it there).

The shirm stick was a wild trip, a psychotic break that left Erin feeling invincible. Like she was a wild animal, and the world was her cage. The guy she'd smoked it with ran off into a residential neighborhood shouting about someone coming down a mountain. The cops were called, but by the time they got there he'd stripped naked and managed to crawl up a telephone pole. There was a lot of yelling. The cops figured he was on PCP. Finally, the guy *slid down the telephone pole*. By the time he got to the bottom he'd loaded up his cock and balls with so many splinters it looked like he had a baby porcupine nestled between his legs. Erin never saw him again, but she heard the stories and figured they were still extracting the splinters from his dick, providing they were able to salvage the thing.

The shirm left Erin feeling particularly insane. She vowed never to do anything like that again. That's when she took up meth. Now speed, that was something Erin liked. She smoked it and the feeling wrapped her up like a warm blanket. It caused her brain to move so fast like doing sprints inside the house even though she was just sitting there. It was amazing. Had more people knew what meth could do for them, the kind of energy they would have, everybody would be doing it. It was life changing.

The door finally opened, and Dr. Scabs came in. In Erin's fragile state of mind, she thought he looked a bit like the rock character from the

Fantastic Four, only more grotesque, considering it wasn't rock, but scabbed over flesh. He had a syringe in hand.

"What's that for?" Erin croaked out the words, practically choking on her dry throat.

"You. You look like you're suffering."

You're okay if you're not seeing bugs. You're okay, girl. You don't need that shit.

Erin shook her head. "I don't touch needles."

"But I'm a doctor. I'm not asking you to wrap your arm with a rubber hose and shoot up like some common junkie. I'm here to help you."

Erin let out a deep breath. *He is a doctor.*

"What is it?" she asked.

"Did you like how you felt? It was euphoria, wasn't it?"

Erin nodded. "Kinda. I guess."

Scabs nodded with her. "Yes, I know. And you were trying to communicate. Do you remember?"

She faintly remembered hearing a conversation Scabs was having with someone else, but she thought it had been in her imagination. She'd even tried to call out, but figured it was all some sort of lucid vision. Kind of like her LSD trips, only ten times more intense.

"You did," Scabs said. "I heard you." He sat down on the couch beside her. "You're a special young woman, you know. Quite honestly, I don't know if it's genes or what, but I do know that my special formula of methamphetamine affects women differently than it does men. But not all women. Only the special ones. Like you. And you've made quite an example of yourself in a very short time." He held up the syringe. "I'm here to take the pain away."

CHAPTER 16

———

Larry and Pizzo walked the perimeter of the house looking for an open window or door, fighting with rose bushes and jacarandas as they did so. They dragged their feet and arms through thick black and brown widow webs, but were too focused on the mission to give a damn. That or perhaps too high. A widow takes a nibble on one of them at it was liable to drop dead from toxic shock.

"Locked up tight," Larry said. "Whoever lives here watches the news."

"What are we gonna do?" Larry scratched a piece of skin from around his corroded nose.

"What do you think? We're breaking into the place. Jesus, that super meth sure has rotted out your brains, hasn't it?"

Pizzo glared at Larry. "Fuck you." Scratched at a particular nasty open sore on his cheek, digging his finger in like a kid finger painting with spaghetti sauce.

They stood in the backyard. Larry surveyed their surroundings. There was a privacy fence, about six feet tall, and foliage that created a decent amount of concealment from neighbors. On top of that, it was the middle of the night. Most everybody was dead asleep.

Larry nodded toward a window beside a sliding glass door at the back of the house. "Aluminum windows. Probably redone in the eighties. This place was probably built with those shitty wooden windows that rise up and always get stuck." He smiled. "It's our lucky day, you speed freak fuck."

Pizzo grimaced at the comment, but his face was so twisted out of shape it was impossible to discern his emotional state through facial expression, much like someone who gets loads of Botox, only the super meth had the very opposite effect as far as beauty went, not that Pizzo was ever a good-looking man or even concerned about his physical appearance.

Pizzo scratched his head. A clump of hair attached to a bit of scabby skin came off. "So, why's this our lucky day?"

"Because these types of windows are ridiculously easy to break into."

Pizzo flicked his hand to get the clump of scalp and hair off almost as if it had offended him.

Larry shook his head. "You're fucking falling apart, man."

Pizzo sighed, which sounded like hydraulic breaks hissing through broken teeth and damaged lips. "It's nothing."

"Bullshit it's nothing. But you go on and tell yourself that. Go ahead and be a slave to Dr. Scabs and that fuckin' super meth. More like super death if you ask me. When we get in here and have things under control you aught to look at yourself in a fucking mirror, man." Using a penlight, Larry shined a beam on the window. "See there. The lock is cheap plastic. Half the time they're broken and just sort of resting in place. It's enough of a deterrent, but I know better. On top of that—" Larry used the palm of his hand to put pressure on the center of the window, where the top and bottom of the aluminum frames met. "—aluminum bends real easy. Just watch it, though. Glass breaks just as easy.

With the center of the aluminum bent and a bit

of finagling, Larry raised the window and gained them access. He smiled. "Easy as Sunday morning."

"How many people we got in here?" Pizzo asked.

Larry shrugged. "Don't know. Probably just one. A middle-aged lady. If she's a widow. Might be a man in there too. Not sure. Hey, you're smaller than me, so you go in and open the sliding glass door."

"I don't wanna go through the window."

"Stop whining like a little bitch and get in there. The quicker you get in there and let me in, the quicker we get this place set up. Scabs wants to get the new hag in here *ASAP*."

Pizzo grunted. He picked at his neck, digging a hole in the flesh with astonishing ease like a woodpecker looking for a grub. "Oh, all right, gimme a boost."

Larry knelt and interlaced his fingers. Pizzo put his foot in Larry's hands, and Larry lifted, overestimating Pizzo's weight, flinging him into the open window with ease. Pizzo made a squelching noise as he slipped into the house effortlessly, crashing over what sounded like a cabinet full of bric-a-brac.

Larry shook his head. "Jesus Christ, you graceless fuck. You're gonna wake her for sure."

Larry heard movement from Pizzo inside. Grunting and groaning. Shifting around through the shattered debris of what sounded like glass trinkets crunching underfoot, muffled by carpeting.

"Come on," Larry said. "Open the sliding glass door." He looked up agitatedly at the other windows, particularly on the second floor. "With all that noise you just about woke up the whole goddamned neighborhood."

A light flicked on upstairs.

"Goddamn it, Pizzo, let me the fuck in. She's up."

The lock on the sliding glass door clicked. Larry grabbed the handle and slung it open, pushing his way in through the fluttering of plastic vertical blinds. Inside, the house was dark. It took a moment for his eyes to adjust. When they did, he saw two things. One, Pizzo had collapsed over a small shelf of those little porcelain figurines with the big eyes that were popular in the seventies (Larry's parents has a pair of them on their dresser that had their names and wedding date on them). Two, he smelled something like burning plastic and realized that Pizzo had already pulled out his glass pipe and was getting a fix of that nasty super meth.

"What the fuck, dude? That shit has rotted your brain for sure. Did you hear me? The lady, providing all we're dealing with is a lady, is fucking awake upstairs. I saw her goddamned light turn on. Get that fuckin' pipe out of your goddamned mouth or I'll shove the motherfucker right up your ass!" Then, under his breath: "Goddamned freak."

Just then a yelp came from the top of the stairs. Both Pizzo and Larry looked up to see a woman standing there in a nightgown.

"What are you doing in my house?" she asked.

"What do you think?" Larry said, smirking. He always liked to see people squirm. It gave him a hard-on.

"Get out of here or—"

"You're calling the cops?" Larry finished. "No need for that. No, there's just a misunderstanding. You see, we're from the cable company. Uh, we're just checking some wires, see." He took a few steps closer to the stairway. "Gotta make sure you can watch the morning news. Let me guess, you get up at, like, five AM, no, four. I bet you get up at four.

Gotta watch the early news, right? Make sure you don't have prowlers in the neighborhood, or, I don't know, thieves."

Larry started up the stairs, slowly.

"You stay right where you are," the lady said.

"Or what? You gonna hurt me? Is that it?"

"I'll call the police!"

"I'll get up these stairs and on your feeble ass before you can get to your fuckin' Jitterbug cell phone and so much as dial the nine one one, you old bitch. Nothing personal, but your house got chosen." Larry shrugged and shook his head. "I'd say sorry, but the truth is I'm not sorry at all. I really couldn't give a fuck less about you or anyone else who might be in this house."

The woman was terrified, shaking violently. This turned Larry on in the strangest way. It wasn't a sexual thing, he wasn't a rapist or anything, and yet he was rock hard. His dick throbbed in his pants. Something about having someone's life in his hands gave him a rush even the best sex couldn't touch. It was a game of cat and mouse. Pizzo was long forgotten. This bitch was his.

The woman revealed she indeed had a phone held tightly against her hip. She held the thing out like a vampire hunter holds a cross out at a bloodsucker.

Larry's eyes deepened with a questioning look. "Holy fuck, you really do have a Jitterbug."

She opened the bulky clam-like flip phone, as if gesturing a threat that would assuage Larry and cause him to retreat in sheer terror. Not a chance. The opposite happened. Larry leapt up the stairs two at a time. The old woman screeched. Scrambling to escape the onslaught of Larry, she dropped her flip phone and twisted her ankle, falling onto the upstairs landing.

Larry laughed. He kicked her phone down the stairs and then used the heel of his boot to kick her in the temple, knocking her out.

"One and done, son," Larry said to himself, or perhaps to Pizzo who was tweaked out in the living room, looking through the woman's stuff, not even paying attention to the fact that there might be other people in the house.

Larry watched Pizzo from the landing upstairs. He fingered through shelves of curios, mostly little hand painted figurines of angels and whatnot. Some of them fell onto the floor and broke. He looked like a child. Well, like some kind of mutant child. Larry shook his head. He checked his watch. They had time. He figured no one else was in the house or they would have heard the commotion. He decided to do a thorough search just in case.

Larry went room to room the way he'd seen cops do in movies. No one else was there. The place looked like it had been locked in the eighties, with the exception of two bedrooms which clearly belonged to teenagers. The only thing plaguing Larry's mind was what if they came home? They would be easy enough to deal with, but what if they were sneaky and saw that something was wrong? Called the police?

He brushed the thoughts away, figuring Dr. Scabs would have already thought about that and had those logistics well taken care of. He didn't pick the hag houses at random. The place had probably been under surveillance for a while, or whatever the method of choosing a new hag house was.

In the kitchen he found a couple of items reminding him of a YouTube video his nephew had watched a few weeks ago.

"Leaning Tower of Pizzo, where are you?"

Pizzo rushed into the kitchen sort of laughing

and grunting. "Look at these! My grandma had ones just like them when I was a kid." He held a pair of slender blue decorative vases. "We could make a killer bong outta one of these."

Larry rolled his eyes. "A bong? Really? What are you, thirteen? I can buy a bong from the fucking head shop."

"Naw, man, it would be cool." Pizzo put one of the glass vases on the kitchen counter beside a half-eaten roll of Mentoes and a plastic bottle of Diet Coke. He stuck his mouth over the opening of the other vase and mimicked smoking weed out of it as if it were a bong. When he pulled his ghastly mouth away, there was the tiny tinkling sound of a couple teeth falling in the vase.

Larry grimaced. "Lost a couple, huh?"

The rim of the vase was slathered in bloody saliva. "Well fuck, I don't have many teeth left, Larry." Pizzo's voice changed a bit due to his new speech impediment.

"No shit, Sherlock. You'll be gumming it in no time. Hey, lookie what I found. Mentoes and Diet Coke."

Though Pizzo's face was an abstract nightmare, there was emotion left in his eyes. The way his twisted brows furrowed told Larry that the poor fuck was confused.

"Come on," Larry said. "I'll show you."

You might as well have a little fun before I put your ass down, Larry thought.

"Better yet," Larry said, "you take this stuff upstairs. Don't eat them or drink the Coke, you hear? I'm serious as a fuckin' heart attack. Believe me, you're gonna want to see what happens. It's gonna be cool as hell. I'll be up in a minute. Just gotta get something from the garage."

With Pizzo upstairs, Larry slipped into the

garage. There was one car, an old Buick, a washer and dryer and some miscellaneous boxes. The walls were adorned with the most meticulous arrangement of tools, nuts and bolts, screws and nails Larry had ever seen. Real old school set up too. Everything had a place.

Larry found a roll of duct tape and a hatchet. He smiled with rush surging through his heart, the way most people feel when they fall in love or come across a valuable collectable in a thrift story.

Upstairs they made quick work of binding the woman's legs and wrapping duct tape around her body, pinning her arms to her sides. She stirred and groaned a bit, but didn't come to.

"What the hell do you have in mind?" Pizzo said.

"Ok, we're gonna do this real quick. You're going to hold her mouth open and I'm going to jam these Mentoes down her throat. She'll probably come to at that point, you know, when she's having a hard time breathing. I need you to maybe straddle her. That might make it a little easier. Just remember to hold her mouth open even if she tries to bite, 'kay?"

Pizzo nodded, then straddled the woman on the bed and grabbed her jaw rather roughly, yanking it open. Larry unloaded the remainder of the Mentoes into her mouth and then used his fingers to push them as far down as he could.

That's when the woman's eyes darted open.

"Hold her tight!" Larry said. His eyes twinkled like a child under the glory of a Christmas tree full of gifts.

Larry uncapped the Diet Coke. "Now I'm gonna pour this down her throat. As soon as I do, you close her mouth and hold it tight. I mean really hold it tight. There's gonna be a lot of pressure there. Got it?"

Pizzo nodded his head enthusiastically.

The old woman squirmed and gagged on the candy. Her eyes bugged out. She tried to move her jaw, but Pizzo had a tight grip. Tears streamed down the sides of her face as she attempted to whip her head back and forth.

Larry gripped the Diet Coke over the woman's head. "Okay, here I go." He poured the coke in and quickly said, "Now close her mouth and hold it!"

The scientific reaction of Mentoes candy and Diet Coke was like adding vinegar to baking soda, only amplified. Just as Pizzo closed her mouth (quite forcefully), a spurt of foam erupted through her lips, and then her cheeks inflated like a big ol' bullfrog croaking in a swamp. It all happened so fast. With nowhere to go, the concoction expanded through her nasal cavity and shot out of her nose in a lava flow of colorful foam. That's when Larry pinched off her nostrils, encouraging Pizzo to, "hold that bitch's mouth shut!"

The gasses from the chemical reaction traveled down her throat and into her esophagus. Her eyes were so wide in her face Larry thought foam was about to spew forth like tears, but then her chest heaved out and he realized what was happening. She convulsed as her insides went haywire.

Larry laughed. He'd dreamed of doing something like this, but never had the opportunity. When he'd killed people in the past, he'd done it out of revenge, and in those instances, though he enjoyed taking the lives, he hadn't really enjoyed the experience. Not like this.

"Watch this," Larry said as he grabbed the hatchet.

Pizzo, still straddling the woman and hunched over, his hand firmly holding her mouth shut, said,

"I can't hold her much longer."

"No worries," Larry said as he took the hatchet and thwacked the woman's bulging neck.

The blade had been kept nice and sharp. The laceration blew out as the pressure finally found a place to escape after being blocked by the woman's organs. A spray of fizzy blood erupted vertically, right into Pizzo's face, which was positioned directly over the woman's neck. When the bloody stream hit him, he flinched and fell backwards. After the initial blowout, her carotid artery pumped a few more times and then it was over.

With the woman's muffled whimpering stifled and the sounds of her struggle eliminated, the room's quiet was only broken by Larry's incessant laughter. This whole operation had been so serious up to this point. He'd been stuck with a goddamned junkie creature with the brains of a baboon. He'd needed this release, and it couldn't have been more glorious and fucked up.

"Jesus fucking Christ!" Pizzo said, wiping bloody foam from his face.

Larry just laughed. "It's an improvement."

"Fuck you. You know, I've had enough of this shit."

Larry brandished the hatchet. "Oh, have you?"

Pizzo wiped goop out of his eyes, nodding. "Yeah, man. That was fucked up."

Larry shook his head. "Have you bothered to look at yourself in the mirror lately? You wanna see fucked up, you're fuckin' ground zero, buddy. No, what's fucked up is that Dr. Scabs went and put me on a goddamned job like this with the likes of you. You're just another piece of street trash."

Raising the hatchet, Larry waited until Pizzo cleared enough of the old Lady's foamy blood from his eyes to see what was happening, then he brought it down on Pizzo's face, directly over his right eye. The blade did some damage, but Larry was kind of shocked that it deflected off the skull. He thought it would dig in like driving an axe into a stump of wood. This action left Pizzo writhing on the ground screaming and clutching his head.

"For fuck's sake," Larry said. He slammed the hatchet into Pizzo head over and over until the thing broke through the skull, embedding itself in mushy brains. When he was finished, his chest heaved and he was out of breath, but satisfied that Pizzo lay there with a fucking hatchet protruding from his cranium like something he'd seen in one of the horror films he so loved when he was a teenager.

In the moments following the murders, Larry was overcome with a familiar feeling, like when he was a kid and would go into the bathroom at church to masturbate.

That feeling was shame.

CHAPTER 17

———

Amber woke to a horrid rank of dried blood and bodily fluids that was masked ever so slightly by old cigarettes and the general funk of the Midtown Motel.

She fully expected to be jolted awake by the police. Waking on her own accord now was quite strange.

The odor hanging in the air quickly brought her brain into reality. The memories of what happened last night assaulted her like a prizefighter's right hook. A man had come into her motel room, and she'd killed him. Well, she'd been forced to kill him. It was self-defense. Dragging his body outside, however, had been a crime.

But I couldn't get through to the police.

So much happened in so little time.

After slipping out of bed Amber crossed the room, careful not to step on the blood-soaked comforter covering the scene of the killing and went to the bathroom. Parched, she drank what little water she had. Though everything that happened last night was crystal clear, there was a weird underlying feeling in the air like waking after a bad drunk or a drug binge and seeing the destruction wrought because of carelessness and excess, something Amber experienced only a few times back in her drug and alcohol days.

What continued to catch her eyes was the comforter on the ground. Blood soaked into it creating a dark stain rimmed with a lighter pink color, almost as if the components of the blood had separated. Perhaps the lighter saturation was the plasma? Amber had no clue. She'd only started to train for a police officer, not a forensics pathologist. Then there was the trail of dried blood leading to the door, like someone dragged a damaged case of chocolate pudding out of the place.

On the other side of that door?

Oh shit, is he still there?

Normally it took a cup of coffee to get Amber going in the morning, particularly in the academy, which had such early mornings, but she found it quite alerting to wake up a murderess who'd tampered with a crime scene. Kind of put a whole new filter on life, one she could have done without.

Unsure of what to do next, Amber decided to get dressed and have her personal items, however few there were, packed and ready to go. It wasn't that she wanted to abandon the murder scene she spent the last night in, which would result in her being somewhat of a fugitive, but that she had no idea what to expect outside. It felt like she was in a motel of the damned where people were torn to pieces by maniac tweakers and no one so much as batted an eye, as if those types of atrocities were common occurrences.

Had things gotten so twisted that she was better off just leaving and hoping there was nothing there to tie her to the crime? No. Definitely not. There was plenty there to tie her to the crime. Her DNA was all over the room, and so was the dead man's blood. Not to mention the register would show she'd been staying in the room where the man was murdered.

Is he still outside the door?

She had to look.

And what if he's not?

Dressed and packed, Amber was ready to face her fate. The strange circumstances of everything that transpired last night, to her, seemed to have altered the course of not only recent events and the search for her sister, but her entire life. There could be cops outside, CSI guys even, though that wasn't likely. There could be dead bodies in the parking lot. There could be one of them right outside the door with a nice black blood trail from a room chock full of her DNA. There was no hiding what had happened, and with such a lapse of time, no way to really prove it had been self-defense.

With a deep inhale, Amber unlatched the door and opened it. What she saw on the other side sent her world even further into the spin it began when her mother called her frantically about Erin gone missing.

On the stoop, outside her room was a mess of congealed human remains. Mostly just coagulated blood, but also something else. Bits and pieces. Problem was that the body had vanished.

Well, all except for the intestines, which were wound through the iron railing like Christmas holly. The eyes dangled from optic nerves, expertly tied—as if that particular method of knot tying was time honored in the Boy Scouts—and hanging from the curly-Q designs on the iron railing. The rest of the body was gone.

In that instant, the only thing Amber could think of was how she was tied to the body. Regardless of her involvement in its mutilation, or lack thereof, considering she hadn't done a damn thing outside of drag the fucker out of her motel room, she would forever be tied to it. In the eyes of the law, the macabre decorations adorning the iron railings was her problem, and what a doozie of a problem that was.

Amber stood almost paralyzed at the threshold of a motel room when the familiar sound of a lighter being flicked caught her attention. At this point she was beyond skittishness and fright. Nothing worse could happen. Nothing could shock her after all she'd been through.

Or at least she didn't think so.

Just outside of the doorway to her neighboring motel room a man, if you could call the creature a man, stood holding a human head like an island tourist holds a drink fashioned from a hollowed-out pineapple. The thing holding the head had a face worse for wear, even more damaged and deranged than that of the man who slipped into Amber's room last night unannounced (of whose head she recognized, cradled in the other man's hands). From the top of the severed head, a length of PVC pipe protruded. From the mouth jutted an old light bulb with some of the glass expertly chipped away as not to shatter the bulb.

Amber recognized a makeshift light bulb meth pipe when she saw one, but why the hell was it jammed in the mouth of a severed head?

Many years ago, Amber learned that you never take your eyes off a drug person, not when they're high enough to climb a telephone pole naked and then slide down the thing like a fireman's pole. And not when they were smoking meth out of a human head.

She descended the stairs slowly only turning to make sure she didn't fall. The man just stood there on the landing sucking in clouds of dope smoke and blowing them out like a chimney, not a care in the world. Amber had never seen someone use drugs so openly. Usually, the people who were doing stuff like meth or heroin were so paranoid, they would lock themselves inside a room somewhere with the windows propped shut and three sets of blinds over them, you know, just in case someone had x-ray vision and could see through the foil they had already taped over the windowpanes.

Once she was on the pavement, Amber realized her heart rate was on high and her body felt shaky from the surge of adrenaline. The man on the landing retreated into his room. This made Amber feel just a smidge more safe, but really anything could be lurking around, and considering the night she had, there was no safety in this godforsaken parking lot of the damned. Life as she knew it would never be safe again.

But what now? Did she even bother checking out of the room? She was a murderer after all, but where the fuck was the body? Well, she knew where the head ended up, but who cut it off? She pivoted to look up at the second floor, certain the body ended up in the room next to hers. They were up there playing with it, making peace pipes out of hollowed out femurs.

Amber shivered at the thought and felt a wave of nausea. She kept her gorge down, for the moment at least. She always had a strong stomach, but how much more of this weird, vile shit could she take?

A sound caught her attention. It came from beneath the stairs. It was a kid's voice, which seemed so out of place, considering the death and violence this motel had seen over the past twenty-four hours.

Craning her head, Amber saw the boy's back. His shirt had a logo that said *Mr. Beast*. Someone in the academy mentioned his kids liked the game, Mr. Beast and some other guy who called himself Unspeakable. Amber felt bad for the kid. Playing under the stairs was probably his only refuge from the madness he was dealing with living in a nasty motel like this. But what could she do for him?

Then, in a gruff voice like kids will use when imitating a bad guy, he said, "I'm gonna get you!" The way he shifted his body made it clear he was playing with toys.

Amber wanted to smile, but couldn't muster even that. It was amazing how a child who had clearly been brought up in terrible circumstances having to play with toys under the stairs at a roach infested crack haven could still disappear into his own world of fantasy. It was a beautiful escapism Amber wished she was still capable of.

Remembering the snacks she had bought yesterday for her stay at the motel of death, Amber pulled a Snickers bar out of her backpack and approached the little boy.

"Hey there," she said as she came closer. "You look like the kind of kid who couldn't say no to a candy bar."

The boy turned toward her as if startled, his motions quick and jerky. It was then that Amber saw he wasn't right. His arms were lanky and too long for his frame, and his head was crooked forward like a buzzard, his eyes protruding from their sockets like the comical image of someone who had been electrocuted. They didn't blink, but stared at her grotesquely, his mouth hanging open as fat bottle flies darted in and out like the kid was a living hunk of garbage.

Stunned, Amber's mouth dropped. She couldn't believe what she was seeing. How had this kid become as mutated and fucked up as the other people she'd seen?

The kid offered a twisted smile, or at least that's what Amber thought it was. He jiggled the things clasped in his rigid, troll-like hands, and that's when Amber realized he was playing with a severed foot and hand, making them do battle like a couple of action figures.

This time she couldn't hold back the urge to vomit. It came out of nowhere, hard and heavy onto the blacktop next to the dark stain of dried blood from the night before. Cigarette butts were jettisoned with the tidal wave of puke like capsized boats. The kid dashed forward, which sent a chill through Amber's spine. She jumped back, not wanting to have to defend herself from a mutant child, but he had other things in mind. He stopped at the edge of the puke and used it as for his beloved toys, dancing the torn appendages in the vomit like Gene Kelly in *Singin' in the Rain*.

The kid laughed as Amber threw herself into her car. It was a horrendous laughter like a kid with a stoma. She peeled out of there as if her ass was on fire.

CHAPTER 18

———

Sitting in his office at the abandoned strip mall, Dr. Scabs waited patiently for the call that the new hag house was prepared and ready for Erin. Her response to the drugs was promising, more so than the other hags he'd housed around town. They had all become mass producers, but she seemed to be transforming at a more rapid rate, which pleased him to no end. He hoped and assumed that meant she would produce at a greater rate as well.

He paused, banishing his thoughts, listening to the hollow ring of an empty mind. There were side effects of the transformation, and those seemed to be far stronger with Erin, one of which was mild telepathy. It was both fascinating and creepy to know the hags could listen to people think and even communicate with them. For all the others it was an anomaly seeming to fade away as their bodies fully transformed. But Erin seemed to accept the changes without abandon in a way the others fought. Certain she wasn't in his head; Scabs continued his reverie.

It had been exciting when Scabs first experimented on his wife Julia, back when his world was crumbling, and she threatened to walk out on him. She'd said it was a purely ethical response to the discovery he'd been using rats, mice and even rabbits to experiment on, all in private, of course. He'd hid the fact he'd been renting out a house turned into a private lab. Julia found discrepancies while going over their finances. Scabs thought everything pertaining to the rental house had been going to *that* mailbox, but somehow, something slipped through. That was all Julia needed to become nosey. She'd thought he was cheating, housing some floozie he was fucking on the side. When she found out it was a place where he treated animals much the way Dr. Mengele treated Jews, she was mortified.

Scabs came home one evening after a long day of injecting animals with his own special blend of drugs and studying their responses when he found Julia with bags packed. She was shocked to see him, clearly expecting to make her getaway before he'd returned. There was even a note she'd planned on leaving. Scabs—at the time he was known by his real name, Edmond Dillenger—became enraged. He acted without thinking, smacking Julia across the face hard enough to knock her out. It was in that moment his life changed forever. All the projects he'd been perfecting were ready for one thing... human experimentation.

He dreamed of human experimentation. Considered using homeless people (there certainly was a glut of them in east San Diego County), but couldn't figure out how he would be able to manage that. In the moment when he assaulted his wife, he knew there was no going back. It was almost as if something in his mind snapped. Consequences just didn't matter anymore. He'd tried his hardest to hide what he'd been doing. He'd been protecting her, and in doing so he hadn't been getting maximum results. He'd been hindering himself.

That night after moving Julia's body to the rental house where his lab was, he developed an itch. It started just below his bellybutton. He'd scratched it incessantly, at first conscious of his efforts and yet unable to stop. Soon enough he was scratching on a wholly subconscious level.

Scratching until he bleed.

Then the area scabbed up and the itch traveled further outward. All the while he experimented on Julia, applying what he'd learned from the multitude of animals he'd poked, prodded and dissected.

His cell phone rang, disturbing his reverie. The ring tone was that iconic two note sound introducing a new scene in any given episode of Law & Order played in a loop (that was just about the only TV show he allowed himself to indulge in, primarily because it could be watched at any given hour since some channel was playing it at any given moment).

"Hello," Scabs said, idly scratching the scabbed over flesh on the back of his neck.

"The house is ready," Larry said. "Had a little casualty. Pizzo was out of his fucking mind. He'd have blown our cover for sure."

Scabs grunted. "He was expendable. We just need to get him to the incinerator. I'm bringing the new hag over right now. She's ready. More than ready. I think she's going to be something very special indeed."

"Yeah, well, everything's in order. You want me to stick around until you get here?"

"Yes. I don't need any unnecessary surprises. I have some... people in mind to work the house. It shouldn't be too long before this hag is producing."

"Alright, I'll be here."

Scabs hung up the phone and left his office to retrieve the new Hag.

***

Erin knew, despite the illusions her mind

provided her, that she was in some locked room somewhere in El Cajon. She knew this and yet she accepted the illusions. It was better to believe in them than to be conscious of how fucked up things had become.

The room was small and cramped, however Erin was on astro-plane of consciousness, stretching to infinity in every direction. It was as if she were slipping and sliding on the folds of a giant tangled brain, grabbing onto the ropey veins for traction. Lightning flashed at times in brilliant bursts of booming thunder, dull and distant like sitting in a quiet movie theater while an action opus plays next door. When the imagery of the everlasting brain was tired, she was flooded with yet another illusion. And then another. And then another. Endless tunnels. Vast forests. Fathomless oceans she could venture without fearing she would drown, for there was no dying in these stretches of absurd illusion. They were the places her mind went. The places her mind got lost in.

The world Erin knew was rapidly losing its cadence and connection. When her hands traveled the physical form, the flesh felt all wrong. It was rough and jagged in places, soft and spongy in others. There was little feeling, as if the nerve endings had been severed. Her mind was the epicenter, and it was on permanent trip through the ethers of the everlasting.

Erin was once a name this creature went by, back in some world this creature was rapidly forgetting. A world without meaning. A world that could no longer convey petty human feelings and emotions on something burrowed into the unused loops of brain matter to something superior, something ethereal, something vast and unlimited.

The door to Erin's tiny domain opened, but the

creature didn't so much as flinch. It could sense Scabs coming. It had been watching him through the astral plane. It wasn't in his head, as it had done when it still identified as Erin, but watched from enough distance that Scabs couldn't detect it. The thing was fully aware of the power of discretion, even though the human traits were almost completely washed away.

"How are we doing, my lovely hag?"

Hag? Why... why is he calling... me... a...

The whiney voice of the one called Erin surfaced within the dreamscape the creature lived. Pesky human emotions caused the final remnants of Erin to spring forth with mindless utterances and useless concerns. The scabbed man could call the creature anything it wanted. That didn't matter, for the creature knew it was more powerful than the scabbed man and his entire army of deformed miscreants. They weren't enlightened enough to travel the astral plane, to see beyond reality. They were just dying flesh, riding a high that would ultimately kill them.

I'm scared!

The creature did not hush or even attempt to soothe the panicked voice of the one called Erin. There was nothing the creature could do for the one it shared a body with. Eventually the Erin consciousness would evaporate, leaving the creature full control of both its mental and physical forms.

There was pressure on the creature's body. Intuitively, it knew to allow the Erin side one last vestige of reality, just to make the transition easier for all involved. The next location would be the final resting place for the physical form, from which the creature's consciousness could roam free.

***

Erin remembered the first time she smoked weed with her best friend Paula. They were thirteen years old. Erin pinched a bud from her sister's stash she found in an old cigar box. In the box were rolling papers, straws, little baggies with a powdery coating, and a couple of pipes. She took one of the pipes and met up with Paula through a little used trail at the back of their local park. They tried the weed, mimicking what they'd seen from movies and heard through the grapevine. When Erin got high the first time it felt as if her mind had floated away from her, only to return to reality in sudden, frightening bursts. It was terrifying at first, but ultimately enjoyable.

Suddenly, finding herself in the tiny break room was a lot like being slammed into reality like on that day she first tried weed, only this wasn't an enjoyable experience. The body her consciousness was trapped in wasn't hers, or at least she didn't recognize it as hers. She had undergone changes. She felt sluggish and lethargic. It was a struggle just to move her arms. Her head felt like it was encased in some sort of heavy metal. With each labored inhale of air she let out wheezing gusts of hot air, and could taste the sweet foulness of her breath.

Lifting one of her arms, Erin examined her hand, waving it slowly from left to right. She'd only done acid a few tines. The trails that followed her elongated fingertips reminded her of that, but it wasn't nearly as amusing as it had been when it was a result of a drug she'd taken for laughs and experience. At this point, Erin couldn't remember why she was there and how things had gotten this bad. She was convinced she'd been drugged, but couldn't figure out why her body looked so different. All she could see were her arms and legs, but they were different. The structure was off, as if her consciousness was encapsulated in another body. The musculature had little definition. The bones had grown. Her knees were knobby knots.

I'm being starved. Someone's holding me in here and they're starving me.

The door opened and a man appeared. He was ugly. Covered in scabbed flesh from head to toe. Even throughout his head where tufts of hair had fallen out or been scratched away and scabbed over. She'd seen him before, but couldn't remember in what context. Considering he was the one on the other side of the door, it wasn't a good context.

Scabs smiled, cracking the scabbed flesh around his lips and cheeks. "How are you feeling today, my dear?"

Erin opened her mouth to say something, anything, but the act of doing such a menial task was more treacherous than she could have imagined. It was as if her lips were sewn shut. She mumbled out an attempt at words. Her tongue darted out, but was blocked by something holding her lips together. Panic rose within. Erin drew forth one of her clumsy and lanky hands, pressing it to her face. She could feel flesh connecting her lips like stalactites stretching from the ceiling of a cave.

"You're special, I'll have you know," Scabs said. "You don't need your mouth anymore. You can talk with your mind. It's quite amazing." He shook his head. "The sad part is that even though I came up with the formula which causes this advancement in evolution, I hardly understand it myself. What I do know is that there is a particular side effect that has revolutionized yet another element of life. Not your life, but that's okay. You are a key piece of the puzzle. You should be honored."

Erin's eyes darted around the room, trying to focus on anything but the scabbed man before her. Anything but the syringe poised in his right hand. Her mind screamed out to fight, but she didn't have it in her to do so. The strength it took to raise her hand and examine the state of her face took everything out of her.

Scabs drew closer. "I can see in your eyes that you are resisting. Don't resist. Enjoy the transformation. You are a special girl. You are going to do amazing things."

Jabbing the needle in her arm, Scabs depressed the plunger. The rush was immediate and welcomed, for it blotted out the pain and confusion Erin had been feeling. It wasn't so much physical pain as it was emotional. Her mind was flooded with random memories like flipping through a photo book without stopping to reminisce. Memories from her youth. Her mother. Her sister. Friends. A life that seemed to have been lived so long ago. A life that was being dissolved.

Erin felt the stuff he dosed her with as it traveled through her arm and into her chest where it hit her heart like a burst of adrenalin, where the drug then shot through her entire body, coating her being like a layer of warm caramel over a scoop of ice cream. She fought to retain her memories, fearing that if she let them go, she would lose them forever. She could sense a dark side to her reality, one embracing the odd new structure of her body, one that would allow her mouth to become sealed shut and welcome the use of her newfound telekinetic abilities.

No!

Scabs nodded. "Yes."

No!

"Oh yes. That's the way. Now we're going to go

for a little drive. I have a place all set up for you. It's a place where the magic happens. You'll like it there. You'll be queen bee. You'll make the calls. You'll also produce a nectar so precious that your minions will do anything for a taste." He leaned in close and whispered into the concave hole in the side of her head that had once been an ear. "You will be god-like."

Erin's chest heaved a few times and then she felt at ease. The serum filled her veins with warm chocolate. Suddenly the idea of being god-like seemed amazing. Suddenly she was connected to an ethereal world she could not see. Her mouth tightened, and though she knew it was closing, possibly forever, she didn't care. Even sounds were challenging as her ear holes tightened up like puckered assholes on the sides of her malformed head. With the sounds of the natural world blotted out, she became aware of an entirely new set of sounds that were always around, but never accessible to the human condition.

At some point Dr. Scabs left the room. He returned with a wheelchair. Through Erin's lazy eyes he looked menacing and horrid, the scabbed-over flesh covering his body in a disgusting crust was like something out of a horror movie. He reached out and grabbed her gently, shifting her to a better position for her to get into the wheelchair. Erin recoiled, not so much in fear, but from the rough texture of his flesh touching hers.

"It's okay," Scabs said. "You still have some of that pesky human emotion left in you. Don't be afraid of me." His eyes glinted. "After all, I'm a doctor."

Erin radiated waves of telekinetic energy. Not words, but raw feeling. She used her mind to encapsulate the space around them with a warmth of sensation, a sort of mental balm to set her changing body at ease for the trip, however Scabs was hit with a wave of that raw feeling. Unprepared for it, he was taken to his knees, hands clutching his head as if the sheer power of Erin's ethereal radiation threatened a head-popping *Scanners* moment.

Sensing she was on the verge of killing Dr. Scabs, Erin pulled back. The uncanny abilities she was discovering were much stronger than she understood. As Scabs rose from his crouched position on the laminate tiled floor, Erin grinned inwardly, feeling a bit like *Carrie* from that old Stephen King book. If she could use her mind to bring Scabs to his knees, what else could she do?

Scabs stood there; his knees bloodied where the scabs beneath the fabric were torn as he was forced to a kneeling position. He stared into the eyes of the creature he'd created, wondering whether he'd done something different to the batch of serum he'd dosed her with or if the results were purely genetic.

Her ethereal voice drifted into his mind: *I'm ready*. And though Dr. Scabs had done this exact procedure with four other strung out junkie women over the past half a dozen months or so, this one truly frightened him. The others were powerful, but Erin was on another level.

Maybe that's a good thing, he thought, and immediately regretted it, considering the creature before him could listen to his thoughts just as clearly as it could deliver ethereal messages.

After helping Erin into the wheelchair, Scabs wheeled her into the loading dock out back where a van waited. He then drove her to the newly acquired house that Larry and Pizzo had secured.

On the ride, Scabs did his best not to think about anything that would disturb or upset Erin, for fear of being zapped by an ethereal shockwave would surely have him jerk the wheel and crash the van. What he thought about as he drove across town was how this would all pan out in the end. After his experiments overwhelmed him to the point of using his own wife as a guinea pig, he'd sort of lost any moral sensibilities he'd been bound by. Somehow his experiments yielded a super meth stronger and far more addictive than any street drug to date. That wasn't what his end game was, but the more he developed the super speed, the more fascinated he was with the results. Particularly the way the addicted were changing. They were like little minions of the hags, only not nearly as powerful. They were walking the streets at night, causing all kinds of problems that the local police couldn't contend with. The little eastern San Diego town of El Cajon was under attack by drug-crazed maniacs and he was responsible.

He scratched his skin incessantly as they neared the house. The scratching was a nervous tick that got the better of him over the past year or so since he'd become completely submerged in his bizarre experiments. It was fascinating to watch his creatures take shape, but it was getting exhausting. And the town was becoming a real dump. He could better live in some beachside ranch in Mexico manufacturing his super meth from an industrial sized warehouse. Have it smuggled into the States and retire on a hammock with the soothing sounds of the ocean to serenade him. Maybe the sun would be good for his skin. Maybe he could dry out the scabs and be a normal human again.

Normal? It was Erin's ethereal voice, and it made Scabs cringe. She'd been listening to the entire time. *What's normal?*

He wasn't sure what that meant, but he tried

hard not to think about anything which might upset her. Thought was the one place everyone had that was truly private. To have the barrier breached was maddening.

By the time they made it to the house, Scabs was thinking again, forgetting his fear of Erin. He wondered if he should do something to sedate her, and immediately regretted those thoughts when his body went numb. He instinctively pushed the brake pedal, stopping the car in the middle of the street. Fortunately, it was a suburban street, the very street on which the house they were heading to was located.

Unable to speak, he sent out direct thoughts. *You don't understand. I'm not trying to hurt you or anything like that. You are very important to me. I need you. This house I'm bringing you to is yours, and you will be able to make anyone here do anything you like. I'm not going to sedate you; I promise.*

After another moment the numbness softened and then went away entirely. Scabs breathed in quick bursts as he drove the car to the house at the end of the street.

Erin recognized the house with a mix of shock and awe.

CHAPTER 19

—·—

After escaping the motel of madness, Amber drove her car into the parking lot of a grocery store. She pulled into the back, away from the cars of people shopping. A few years ago, she would have pulled into a similar—perhaps even the very same—parking lot to score dope. Even thinking of the past sickened her almost as much as what happened at the motel.

The realization that her future in law enforcement was completely squashed created a deep chasm in her soul, but it was still overshadowed by her determination to find Erin. Maybe this was her last chance to save Erin. If her efforts proved inconsequential and Erin succumbed to the life of a junkie, at least Amber tried. That's all she could do. If her efforts failed, she would have to go her own way and hope Mother could accept which she could not control.

Grabbing her phone from a little pocket stitched on the inside of her purse, Amber checked the charge, surprised to see she had fifty percent. With everything that had gone on, she'd forgotten to put her phone on the charger like she did every night.

She had a few calls to make. First, she dialed her mother's house, but the line was busy, which wasn't all that surprising. Mother still had a landline and always gabbed to her sisters and a couple of friends. Amber remembered how frustrating that had been when she was a teenager. Amber's incessant complaining about the line being busy eventually caused her mother to breakdown and buy her a cell phone. Next, she dialed her mother's cell, figuring if she were on the land line, she would eagerly answer hoping Amber decided to help on the intervention with Erin. Her cell went straight to voicemail. Again, not something to be concerned with, but unusual. Her mother charged her cell regularly, hardly using the thing enough for the battery to wear out and lose a charge quickly. In fact, Amber couldn't remember a time that her mother's cell phone was turned off or dead.

On a whim she tried Erin's cell, but it was dead as well. That's what really brought on a feeling of dread. A young woman was not without her cell phone. Erin's generation was raised on those things. They lived by them. The lack of social media activity and a dead cell were major red flags. Bad signs for sure. Kids without cell phones were dead in ditches or wandering the streets, and really nothing made sense outside of Erin having gotten a new phone with a new number, which was a real possibility. The best way to push your loved ones away was to completely disconnect from your old life.

Amber put the phone down and closed her eyes. She wanted to cry, but was too frustrated for tears. She'd cried last night as she fell asleep. She'd cried for her sister, her mother, and for the fact that she'd been forced to murder a man.

A pounding on the driver's side door window startled a quick scream from Amber, thrashing her out of deep thought. Pivoting her head to the left, she caught sight of a sorry looking woman with her hands open and splayed across the glass, a cigarette pinned between two of the fingers of her right hand. Her face was all red, like she was deep into cirrhosis. Boils and pustules dotted her face like a gross-out version of Connect the Dots. Her eyes were so red they looked like they were drenched in blood.

The woman's words, muffled through the closed window, but legible enough even with her sloppy speech impediment and lack of teeth, came out in a staccato burst. "Hey, you got any dope? You got some of that super-duper meth? Do you? Do you? Well DO YOU?!"

Amber flinched as the woman's voice raised there at the end. She expected the woman to pound on the window. *Give me my fucking meth!*

Amber just shook her head, her sad eyes staring into the bloody depths of this poor woman's addiction. *Jesus Christ I hope Erin isn't this far off*, Amber thought.

The woman's eyes narrowed. "You holding out on me?"

Again, Erin shook her head.

The woman pulled her hands away, leaving grimy smears on the window. She placed the cigarette in her mouth and sucked in a deep drag. Erin saw now that her neck had an almost scaly quality to it, like a reptile. After pulling the cigarette away, the woman exhaled without opening her mouth. Smoke seeped in tiny tendrils from rips and tears along her cheeks and neck, engulfing her face in a blue haze before rising off her head.

Cringing, Amber made sure the locks were down and then she put her car into gear.

"You have some, don't 'cha!" the woman said. "Give it to me! You're holding out, you bitch!"

A hundred feet further Amber had to slam the breaks to avoid hitting a tweaker on a bike. He was riding with his hands crossed over his chest, back straight like a board. She cringed looking at his face, and then realized he was so hideous because his lower jaw was gone. Just an open cavity with a tongue lolling out, flapping in the wind. There were only a couple of teeth left embedded in his upper jaw like rancid corn kernels. His eyes were sucked deep into their sockets like his brain was shriveling up and tethering them inward by the optic nerves. The man swiveled his head erratically, swooping and swerving on his bike, but managed to keep it straight and rolled on by.

Uncertain where to go, Amber's mind kept returning to a particularly bad dope house she used to frequent on Second Street. The house had been known as Heaven House, mostly because they sold a great deal of heroin back in the day. That had never been Amber's drug of choice. They also sold weed, meth and whatever else the people who lived there got a hold of. She remembered going in and seeing people sprawled out on the couches having just shot up. After the initial euphoria wore off and the fear of withdrawal was eliminated, they would leave and shoot their dope elsewhere. She'd never spent a lot of time there, really. Just bought her shit and moved on. But the place was notorious. If someone in the house recognized her, she might be able to get some good info. Maybe someone there would remember her sister. Chances were, Erin had been there.

CHAPTER 20

———

As the van pulled into the driveway of the new hag house, the garage door opened. Inside, Larry stood waving Dr. Scabs in. After a quick maneuver to back the van into the garage, the door closed again. The act was so quick and natural that the neighbors would have absolutely nothing to concern themselves with.

As the van cooled and ticked, Larry helped Scabs take Erin out of the back.

"So, everything's ready?" Scabs said.

Larry nodded. "Yep. We'll set her up in a room upstairs. We haven't had any surprises since we got here."

"Good. Help me get her into the wheelchair."

Larry helped Scabs pull Erin out of the back of the van, cringing as his skin touched hers, which was all soft, squishy and almost rancid looking. He made an ugly face and shuddered.

"She's molting," Scabs said. "Or at least that's the best way to explain it. Her change has been a lot quicker than the others."

"Nasty."

Scabs narrowed his eyes at Larry. "Nasty, huh? She's going to help produce the finest meth this town has ever seen. I have a good feeling about this one. I think we've found our gold standard."

Larry held Erin steady as Scabs pulled the wheelchair out of the van and prepared it. "I miss the old stuff, to be honest."

The comment caused Scabs to hesitate. "Old

stuff? What the hell are you talking about?"

"You know, good old ice. Even the real strong shit that would keep you up for three days. I mean, it could be a little scary especially if you saw the goblins," Larry chuckled, "but, you know, it was a great high."

Scabs offered a grim stare. "You saying my stuff isn't great?"

"I'm not saying that at all, it's just," Larry stammered, "It's just I kind of miss the old stuff, that's all. Like, you know, for nostalgic reasons, and shit." He shifted Erin's body. She wasn't too heavy, but the feeling of her flesh disgusted him. "Can we get her in the wheelchair, man?"

Scabs opened the wheelchair and then Larry gently placed her in its cradle. He shivered afterward, using the bottom of his t-shirt to quickly wipe away the residue her skin left on his bare arms.

"She can sense your reaction, you know," Scabs said, scratching at an ornery scab over his left shoulder. He'd been nervous all day, scratching even more than normal. His white dress shirt was stuck to his torso in several places with stains of red and orange drying blood. He grinned. "She's a strong one, too. You know how women can be. She starts thinking you're repulsed by her, and she might get upset."

Larry looked at Erin in the wheelchair. "That's hardly a woman anymore."

"You know, Larry, you look like you need a pick me up. I have some guys coming here to help with further preparations. We get her set up, I figure she'll start producing in no time flat. I think she's going to be a super-producer. But I need everyone on their game. They get here, I want you to get some of the latest batch from Second Street house."

Larry got really quiet.

"Looks like you haven't had any in quite some time."

"Like I said, I miss the old stuff. Can't hardly find it anywhere anymore."

"That's right. What's the problem, Larry? Don't like my stuff. It's far more potent than the old ice shit. What's not to like?"

"Forget it. Let's wheel her in and get her set up."

"You know, I'm beginning to think you haven't been sampling the supply you've been selling. That's a requisite, you know. Anyone who works for me must sample the supply. You have to know what you're selling."

"I know what I'm selling."

"Do you really?"

Larry nodded. "Yeah, and I don't have to like it. I'm just making a buck, man. Fuck, isn't it better I don't sample my supply? That means I'm selling more."

Scabs gripped the handles of the wheelchair tight. "Look, you either take the shit or you get the fuck out, only way I see it there's just one way out." They both heard a car pulling up. "There's your help. They have materials for the hag setup and at least a few pounds of product. You smoke up or you're going to end up like your pal Pizzo."

"That's just it. You want me to become one of your fucking dope zombies like Pizzo. That's just a slow death anyway. Fuck that, man."

Scabs shrugged. "Have it your way. See what I care. Your type is a dime a dozen on the streets, and everybody's using the stuff I'm selling, so there's no shortage of people who would love to work for me just to take a little bit off the top. I don't need you."

Scabs pushed the wheelchair to the door that went into the house, pulled back to allow the front wheels to catch on the threshold and then pushed Erin in.

***

The voices swam in and out of Erin's consciousness, but she couldn't be bothered to give a damn what they said. It was someone else's argument. But what really got her was when she was being pushed again. She was rolled into a house and hit with a smell so familiar it gave her the most peculiar sense of deja vu. It was one of those smells caught fleetingly that reminded her of something from the past. She couldn't put her finger on it, like a perfume triggering some deep emotional response, if only for a moment.

Deep down in a body that had taken on a severe transformation, her heart yearned for something within the house which was intimately familiar, but she couldn't place it, as if there was a barrier up keeping her from memories.

As Scabs pushed Erin through the house, she tried desperately to remember who she was. It was as if her mind didn't work properly, and that frightened her. Waves of panic rose only to be stifled by tides of calm, flowing through her body like reassuring waves of absurd peacefulness. She would stop and listen to the thoughts of those around her. Scabs was an insane man, that was clear by the nonstop rambling in his head. He had mental ticks. Words flashed through his mind like bright fluorescent lights in Vegas. And yet he seemed to compartmentalize these maddening and frequent flashes of thought, pushing them to one side of his consciousness, the other side well trained and focused on the task at hand. Currently his focused side contemplated getting her up a flight of stairs. The mad side of his brain fought for purchase, but he kept it pushed off to the side like he'd been living with this mental affliction for so long, he was quite comfortable in his sick head.

"Give me a hand with her," Scabs said, but Erin didn't know whom he was talking to, nor did she care.

Scabs and another man hefted her up the stairs. They brought her to a room and once again her nostrils were assaulted by a smell so familiar it threatened tears from her monstrous eyes. It was a reaction she couldn't control, some deep emotional response she didn't quite understand, and yet she understood one thing perfectly well.

She was home.

What she didn't understand was whether she was in a new home or back in the home from a past she'd been trying desperately to forget, a past erased from her mind. Even thinking about her childhood left her feeling sour and used up. It was better to float away into the nothingness of her bizarre new reality. Accept the change.

Erin's consciousness floated off and she sensed others like her, but at the moment was too afraid to make contact. She rushed back to the house in which she currently resided, the one which elicited fragmented memories of a past she thought was completely lost. There were voices around her. Laughter. Things were happening. Things were being constructed around her, for her. When she slipped into the minds of these sad men who worked feverishly at construction resembling a science lab (or better yet a bizarre meth lab), she almost pitied them for their brainlessness. They were idiots. Mindless junkies who burned holes in their cerebrum by smoking crystal meth, the new shit. Erin almost felt bad thinking down on them since she was a user herself, but she was so far above them now that she just laughed inwardly. Her body heaved a bit, which startled the men. Clearly her new form, the mutation came over her so rapidly, turning her into an unsightly creature, was something they feared, and for that she tried to move even more, finding the very act of movement to be quite a task.

"The fuck is she doing," one of the men said. His mouth gaped, revealing wasted gums and a couple shards of a black tooth like burnt planks of wood.

The other guy just shook his head. "Fuck if I know. Let's get this shit finished and get the fuck out of here. These fuckin' hags are creepy as shit, dude." Tweaker number two had pockmarked skin and deeply sunken cheeks thin enough in some areas that he'd scratched holes in the skin. Only a day ago he was convinced his tattoos were coming to life, and thus scratched one off his arm before realizing he was just way too fucked up.

The first tweaker raised his eyebrows. "You're one to speak. You're fucking' creepy as shit, bro."

"Hey, fuck you!"

Curious about what she was capable of, Erin spoke gently into the tweakers' minds. *You think I'm creepy, is that it?*

Both shared a look of sheer fright. "What the fuck was that?" one of them said. The other just shook his head.

*What the fuck do you think it is? I can see your every thought, you sick fucks. I can see everything, every experience, every crack whore you let give you a nasty, toothless blowjob, every dog you kicked out of spite, every time your disappointed your family, when Katie left you—*Gart, the one with the scabbed-over tattoo gaped at this particular comment *—the kids you abused, the* *people you ripped off, the dicks you sucked for more dope—*

Gart looked at his buddy with questioning eyes. Jerry stammered, "It was just one time. I was hard up. You know how it is."

At least three times. One time you took a load in your mouth, panicked and swallowed.

"You fucking bitch!" Jerry said, anger rising from within. He took two aggressive steps toward Erin, arm raised with a tube of thick glass in his hand from the lab, but before he could clock her in the head like he wanted to, she put a grip on his brain he'd never felt before. It was as if an invisible hand reached into his head and squeezed.

Jerry collapsed, weeping, and crying on the carpet. The absurd form that once was Erin trembled, sick laughter gurgling from deep down in her throat. Gart said, "Fuck this shit," and fled the room.

Moments later, Dr. Scabs entered the room. He ignored Jerry on the floor and went straight to Erin. He stood there a moment, staring at her. "What did you do?" He finally craned his head and looked at Jerry writhing on the ground.

Erin remained silent. Though she was becoming increasingly aware of her power, there was something about Scabs that intimidated her. It was as if she knew he'd created her, which meant he probably had the ability to destroy her. Then again, she thought she could destroy him just as well. She slipped into his mind, but only for a moment. The madness therein was far too much for her to handle. It was impressive how he could live with a mind so fucked up and remain composed.

I toyed with their minds. Erin could only stand to speak in short sentences with Scabs. The less time spent in his mind, the better.

"Well, don't." He stared at her a moment, and Erin wondered if he was processing his own madness to find the right words. She wondered what would happen if he were to allow the crazy side of his mind to take over.

He stared into her jaundiced eyes almost like a lover. "You are special, my dear." His mouth tightened. "Just don't fuck it up. Things like this keep happening and I'll have to sedate you. Heavily."

Scabs walked out of the room.

Jerry lay on the floor unmoving.

Erin reflected on what transpired. The man in the room with her was probably dead. She'd used mental prowess to squeeze his brains. If she had that kind of power, who could stop her? Dr. Scabs?

What stuck in her consciousness the most was the voice in which she spoke to Jerry and Gart. It was a soft, feminine voice. A voice as familiar as the smells she recognized when entering the house.

As she sat there in her new domain, she noticed movement from the shadows. She seemed to exist during human reality and some unseen plane. She saw both places simultaneously, as if living in some sort of double exposure. She could go to one or the other as she pleased, but she liked seeing both places at once. From the shadows, figures emerged. Erin couldn't tell where they really came from or who they were, but they beckoned to her as if she were a beacon. Deep down her human consciousness said, *shadow people. If you see them or bugs, you're too far gone.*

The monstrous side of Erin accepted the shadow people as they came to her. They stood around her as if in awe, awaiting instruction. A grin surfaced on Erin's face, a twisted sort of thing looking more like a grimace.

CHAPTER 21

—·—

Amber drove by the house on Second Street four times before pulling into the driveway. She'd made excuses in her head, but the only thing holding her back was fear. She'd been to this particular drug den many times in the past, but returning now that she was on the other side of the law felt like she was entering enemy territory preparing to conduct an undercover sting. Something she wasn't even close to being prepared for. Rookie cops didn't do this kind of shit. Most veterans didn't have the intestinal fortitude to go undercover.

Before exiting the car, she looked at herself in the rearview mirror. The events of the past forty-eight hours took a toll on her. She looked ragged. Her eyes were red and puffy, her complexion splotchy, hair a mess. She grinned and said to herself, "You look like you belong here."

Walking up to the door Amber was hit with vivid flashbacks of taking the very walkway so many times when she needed dope. When she needed refuge from the wicked realities of the real world. When she needed the comfort of those she once fooled herself into believing were friends. The debris littering the outside of the house was stacked twice as high, but the cracks in the concrete walkway were the same. The flaking paint on the porch showing through to no less than four previous colors was the same. The big difference was the trepidation, the fear. In the past she only feared that no one would let her in, or they would be out of meth (something that rarely ever happened). Now her fears were more substantial.

She stood there at the front door a moment mentally gathering her facilities. Taking deep breaths. Reminding herself of what she was there for. This house was dangerous. Even when she stopped by in the past for refuge, it was a dangerous place. She was just too stoned and lost to give a fuck. There were most certainly guns in there. Plenty of deceit, lies, drugs. People had likely been murdered in here at one point or another. She'd seen a man beat near death once. Laughed in his bloody face. His only infraction was that he owed twenty bucks for some dope. Three men served him up hockey style and kicked his teeth in. Amber was loaded off her ass and found the whole thing to be quite a rush.

Thinking back, she was embarrassed to have been that person. So cold. So wasted away. On the verge of completely losing herself to not only the drugs, but the lifestyle. She feared her sister was on the same path. Further on the path. She hoped Erin wasn't too far-gone to be helped.

After one final deep breath, Amber rang the doorbell. She suddenly wished she'd taken drama back in high school. This was going to be the performance of her life. On the other hand, all she had to do was slip into the woman she'd once been. She most feared she wouldn't be able to fool them. If they smelled a rat, she could be the one on the end of a severe beating, and it would be her sister laughing as her teeth were kicked in.

The two by four-inch peep latch on the door swung open. Amber let the features on her face slacken, her mouth left open slightly to achieve what she hoped would be a look of despair.

The eyes seen through the peep were striped with red and purple capillaries like little lightning bolts, some of which were blown out like red ink on super absorbent paper. The flesh around the eyes looked pink and swollen with a juicy sheen like the guy had been crying pus or his face had been slathered in oil.

"Yeah," he said, his voice gruff.

"It's Amber. I—I haven't been here in a while. I need some stuff. Like real bad."

The eyes narrowed.

Amber ran a hand through her greasy hair and shifted around, eyes darting to the left and right, hoping she looked like a girl who was fiending for a fix. "Look, I used to come here all the time. I know Larry and Pizzo. They still hanging around here?"

The eyes brightened up. "Larry and Pizzo, huh?"

The sound of several locks being unlatched issued, and then the door opened. This was her last chance to get out. Amber could turn and high tail it to her car, jump in and back out of the driveway, get the fuck out of there. Yes, she could do that, but then she would be giving up on Erin. She'd been told by experienced cops that training was good and all, but mostly it was like reading textbooks and memorizing procedure. The real training started once a rookie was on the streets. Sure, Amber was jumping a few years of training, but here she was. It was all or nothing.

The man who opened the door was no man at all. He was a monster. His face looked like Jeff Goldblum's during his transformation in the *The Fly*. His flesh was infected and oozing pus. His nose was gone, two little holes remaining, and his ears were on their way out. One side of his head was just a hole with hairs sticking out. The ear he had left resembled a mushroom.

The sight of the man almost caused Amber to panic. Pushing her fears aside, Amber stepped into the house. She'd seen others like him. The night people at the motel, for instance. It was the result of the super meth. It was literally killing people, but in an entirely different way than drugs had killed users in the past. It was breaking down their bodies.

"I'm Leche," the man said. "Pizzo and Larry are off at other houses. Or dead." Leche laughed at that sentiment. His lips were splitting like rubber on sun-baked tires. As he laughed, viscous fluid escaped his throat and dribbled out of his mouth. He used his green tongue to sort of lick it up, and then spit a wad of infected goop on the floor.

At this, Amber felt her gorge rise, but kept herself under control.

"Chill out here for a minute," Leche said. "I got some of the new batch in. It's really fucking good."

Something caught Leche's eyes. He was moving around like he was under water, his motions fluid-like. He knelt and grabbed a glass pipe from the coffee table, adorning a grotesque couch in the sitting room. The end of the pipe was broken, but he didn't seem to mind when he shoved it into his mouth and used a lighter to run a flame beneath the bowl, which was already blackened from previous use. He made obnoxious sucking noises and sort of twisted the broken end of the pipe in his mouth, grinding what was left of his lips. Amber cringed as she watched him mutilate himself.

A tiny puff of smoke rose from the bowl. Leche sucked in, a wheezing sound coming from his throat, and then pulled the pipe away in grand fashion, heaving his chest out as he held the smoke in his lungs. He held the pipe out as an offering. Amber shook her head. There was no way for her to hide the disgust on her face. Leche's mouth was a wet wound oozing blood. When he finally exhaled, blood droplets sailed through the air in the puff of dope smoke. Amber shifted quickly to the left, avoiding being sprayed.

Leche laughed. "Kinda grabs you by the booboo." He dropped the pipe onto the soiled carpet and turned, walking zombie-like out of the room.

Suddenly feeling completely out of her element and in over her head, Amber took in the room for the first time since returning. She'd sat in that very room many times before, so high she thought she could kiss the sun. She'd had what she once perceived as great times in the room. Wasted time. Lost hours, days, months.

But it wasn't as bad back then, or at least she didn't remember it being as bad. The very couch she used to sit on was now putrid. There was no telling what the thing was coated with, but it appeared sticky. If this place had more like Leche who were rotting away, then she imagined what the couch was saturated in. The coffee table was a mess, but that was nothing unusual. The smell of the place was enough to make her want to puke. Drug houses always smelled bad, but this was another level of funk. It smelled as if the house itself were an organic thing, rotting from the inside out.

Everything in Amber's mind told her to get the fuck out of there. This was no place for her to be. She was in danger. It was a foolish idea to think she could go undercover and find her sister. She should have just gone to the police.

What, have them find out you killed a man?

That would be better than this.

A sound from the hallway just off the front door

caught her attention. She looked up to see something emerge. The house was lit very dimly with old lamps and candles, creating deep shadows from which the thing reared itself. The body was human in shape, but off kilter. The limbs were too long, the hands hanging down past the thing's knobby knees. The fingers were like claws from the grotesque Nosferatu version of Dracula. It wore no clothes, its skin a sheen like it was wrapped in plastic. When the thing was fully in the sitting room Amber could plainly see that the face was merely a skull wrapped in skin. No nose, no ears, no lips. The grimace was ghastly, the eyes too far apart, the cranium overlarge. No teeth, just wet gums the color of spoiled meat.

Amber's first reaction was fear, but the thing paid her little mind, electing to sit on the couch, which made a disgusting wet squelching sound as its misshapen body made contact. The thing hunched over, it's greenish tongue darting over the vacant gums, its breaths heavy and labored.

Amber stood there shaking. She'd never seen anything like this. It was distinctly human in form, and yet the thing was alien. It was creature.

It's what the other guy is turning into. What they're all turning into.

The tweaker creature slowly swiveled its oblong head to face Amber. The eyes protruded from its skull like little ping pong balls had been pushed in there. The capillaries were so thick and engorged with blood they gave the orbs texture. The color was gone, the pupils so dilated they were like black holes completely obliterating any color to the irises.

The thing licked its gums as it stared at Amber. She couldn't even begin to wonder what it must have been thinking. Was it turned on? Did it want to kill her?

Leche returned with a cigar box in hand. Amber couldn't help but stare at his mouth, the way the blood was drying. It looked painful, and yet he didn't seem to notice. He must have been so high, pain wasn't an object anymore. Amber remembered a time when she would have loved to get that high. Not at this expense, though.

"Ah," Leche said, "one of them decided to join us."

One of them?

"Would you like a treat?" Leche asked the creature.

The creature nodded its head, tongue dangling further like a hungry dog. Saliva dripping out of its mouth, nothing there to keep it in. It didn't seem to care as thick ropes of drool dripped onto its malformed chest (the musculature, much like the rest of its body, was all wrong, almost tumorous in nature, like the muscles had fissured and split, fighting for purchase beneath stretched skin and bulging at the weak points).

Leche set the cigar box on the table and opened it up. He pulled out a chunk of meth that must have been a couple grams. Amber would have sucked the Devil's dick for a chunk like that back in the day.

Leche looked at her. He still had some humanity left inside, mostly in the eyes. She could almost read him. Not humanity in the morality department. Humanity rather than barbarism like the thing on the couch.

"They can't smoke or snort anymore," Leche said. "So, we have a new way to administer their medicine." He looked back at the creature. "Open wide."

The creature's disgusting maw grinned hideously, its tongue slapping around the wet rotting orifice. Amber watched in horror as it slouched its lanky body down onto its back, lifting its legs into the air. Where its crotch should have been was a thick scabbed mass, below which its asshole puckered like a sea anemone. At this foul display, Leche grimaced as if his own body wasn't slowly decaying like this creature, and he too wouldn't soon be engaging in such uncouth activities.

Leche handed the thing a fat rock of super meth, of which the creature plucked greedily. Wasting no time and sparing no dignity, the creature crammed the rock of meth up its ass, pushing it in until it was two knuckles deep, like inserting a suppository. With the dope rock swallowed up, the creature switched back to a normal sitting position. It's rotten looking body quivered, bug eyes bulging even further (there were no eyelids to speak of, thus they rolled around to remain moistened from the leakage around their swollen sockets). Its mouth hung limp, tongue lolling out like a dead serpent.

Amber thought the thing had overdosed. But then its chest heaved in and out violently. Hot, foul breaths escaped the gaping mouth in rancid gusts.

"He'll be like that for a while. Then he'll get the fuck up and help with production until he needs another dose." As an afterthought, Leche added: "And then he'll die." Again, as if he himself wasn't on the same path.

The urge to flee was strong, but Amber knew that would appear suspicious. Leche would be after her, and if he got his hands on her she wouldn't make it out of the house alive.

"Now for you," Leche said.

He pulled a glass pipe out of the box (it was fully intact, but heavily used by the look of the jet-black bowl). He extended the pipe to her. After

Amber didn't immediately accept his offer, he said, "Or do you prefer shooting?"

Oh fuck.

"Well, really I came here looking for someone."

Leche tilted his head. "You can do a line if that's your thing, chica."

Amber bit her lip. She could kill time by crushing up a line, but then she would have to do it.

She did *not* want to do a line.

"I'm looking for my sister."

Leche's eyes narrowed. He scratched his face, peeling away little bits of skin and chewing on them nervously.

Erin continued, "Maybe you've seen her here. She's got a bad habit. I'm sure she's been through here."

"Smoke, shoot, or line? Choose one."

Amber drew in a breath and held it there. *He's not going to let you go until you do one. You're fucked, girl.*

She let out her breath and said, "Line. I'll chop."

Leche shrugged and pulled a small chunk of crystal from the box. He used his palm to clear a spot on the table and placed it there.

Stay in character. You're slipping and he can tell. Just do the line. Make it small. You've done this shit before. Just deal with it.

Amber plucked a credit card from the debris on the table and went to work crushing the rock into powder, asking questions as she worked on it.

"Her name is Erin. She looks kind of like me, but she's a teenager. You seen her?"

"I see a lot of people in here. I don't remember no one. No one but the regulars."

"She might have been a regular."

Leche shrugged. "Things have been changing, chica." He leaned in. "I've been changing." His eyes darted to the creature on the couch. Leche grinned. "That motherfucker changed *a lot*. And there's more like him. A lot more."

Amber became nervous at the prospect of snorting the line. She kept on crushing it beneath the credit card, trying to spread it out so she could make a tiny little line and fool Leche, but he was on her like a buzzard to roadkill.

"Why are they like that?" Amber gestured to the creature (still lost in a drug haze unlike anything she'd ever experienced with speed). "Like him?"

"It's evolution, but at a sped-up rate. It's the change."

"He doesn't look happy."

"Oh, what you don't know. He's fucking happy. He's on fucking cloud nine, man."

"What about my sister? You sure you haven't seen anyone that looks like they could be related to me. I think she had her hair dyed purple last time I saw her, but that was months ago. Who knows?"

"You gonna snort that shit or just fuckin' play with it?"

She decided to make two lines, start with one, and hope she could get out of there before he forced her to do the second one.

Leche watched her intently.

Amber grabbed a cut of straw on the table and flicked it away in disgust after realizing it had blood on it. From her purse she pulled out a dollar bill and rolled it up. *Just like the old days. You're only doing this to stay in character and get out of here with your life. That's it. Don't freak out.*

Amber knelt and sniffed a line up her right nostril. She thrust her head back, just as she used to do. The feeling was so sickeningly familiar, almost comforting for just a split second as the adrenaline bomb shot up her nasal passage and radiated through her body. She became hyper aware of everything, every sound, the heavy breathing of the tweaker creature on the couch, the soft chuckle emanating from Leche's mouth, a TV that was on somewhere else in the house.

She wanted to deny how wonderful it felt, but couldn't. It was like sitting in a favorite chair, or putting on a warm sweater, it was familiar in all the wrong ways. Comforting, even in a shithole house with some fucking monster on the couch and a man who kept scratching chunks of skin off his face and chewing on them.

"With the women it's different," Leche said. "I get the feeling you haven't done this new shit yet. You look green. You look like you ain't never done a line in your life, but I can tell you have. You know what to do. This sister of yours, I've seen her. She'll bump uglies for some rock, I'll tell you that."

Amber's eyes narrowed. The rush her body experienced was such that she almost lunged forward and attacked Leche, but she held it together. Her heart rate could have kept up with a death metal drummer at that moment. Leche's comment did nothing to help.

"Where is she? Is she here?"

Leche shook his head. "Like I said, it's different with the girls who take this stuff. Some of them anyway. Some go all nasty like this guy over here. I don't even remember his fuckin' name. But some show potential. Those ones, well, they can produce. We call it *Mother's Milk*, but that ain't what it is. Don't get it twisted. Their bodies change and they produce the purest form of this shit." He shook the cigar box. "It's fucking incredible. You're sister, she's a producer. A queen. You see, when they change, they get all nasty, like I said, and we call 'em hags. Even this motherfucker right here. He's just a hag now." Leche chuckled. "He don't even have a dick. Can you believe that? Your sister is a queen bee in a hag house somewhere in town. Word is she's special."

Amber was shaking badly. She looked at the hag creature on the couch. He was stirring from his daze. "Does she?"

"Look like that?" Leche shrugged. "Fuck if I know. All I know is you do look like her, and I thought you *were* her when I saw you outside, last I heard she was hagged out. How you feelin', chica? Pretty good?"

Amber just sort of shook her head, which was spinning. A deep feeling of shame swelled from within, as if she had taken the drugs on her own accord. As much as she tried to reassure herself this was merely a means of survival, there was a part of her conscience reprimanding her decision, as if there had been some other way to deal with the current situation, of which there wasn't.

"I'm feeling good," she said, attempting to remain in character. At this point, even though the high itself was just as good as she remembered, she was feeling like complete dog shit. She wanted to puke, as if by doing so she would purge the drug from her body. But she knew better. Depending on how good the stuff was she would be dealing with the high for a while. Hopefully the comedown wouldn't be too bad since she'd done such a small amount, but she wasn't crossing her fingers. For such a small line she was out of the stratosphere.

"Have the other one," Leche said. "We got plenty. The hags are great producers."

Amber shook her head. If she took the other hit, she feared there was no coming back. She already felt like crawling up the walls. If she took more, she'd tear her own skin off and paint portraits with her blood.

"I insist," he said.

"I gotta go."

Leche tilted his head questioningly. *Leaving so soon?*

Amber nodded. "I'm not feeling well. I just stopped in to ask about Erin anyway. You sure she's not here?"

"Sure as shit. But hey, don't leave so soon. Take that line, it'll perk you up."

"Oh, I'm plenty perked up. Just not feeling good."

"That's because you need some more. Take the edge off. You're only halfway there, chica. You gotta go all the way."

Amber rose from the chair she'd been sitting in. On her left the tweaker creature shifted, which caused her a moment of pause. It was such a reactionary movement the thing made; she was worried it would go after her like a vicious dog.

"Don't worry," Leche said, "he won't bite." Leche laughed. "He ain't got no teeth."

Amber made quick steps toward the front door, but Leche quickly positioned himself in her way.

"You ain't going nowhere," he said.

Grabbing a three-foot glass bong, she'd been eyeing on the coffee table, Amber swung it like a bat into Leche's face.

"Fuck you!" she screamed.

CHAPTER 22

Eventually Erin drifted off into the ethers as a team of haggard creatures, many of which weren't as cretin-like as others, worked on her throne, as Dr. Scabs called it. It was fascinating how far away from her body she could travel through the invisible ethereal vapors streaming through the world, unseen avenues rife for mind travel that humans weren't capable of.

As she passed houses, she heard thoughts like listening to a large crowd and getting fragments of various conversations. She would stop and listen from time to time. People thought of such mundane and boring things. Lovers, work, finances, epic dreams of fame and fortune. Revenge. Those were the most entertaining thoughts to pry upon. Some people dreamed of revenge as much as others dreamed of sex.

Soon enough she grew bored of the mental pathways and returned to the house where she found her physical form in a compromising, and yet not completely uncomfortable position.

Scabs was shining a light in her eyes. Once she returned to her brain, she closed her eyes violently to avoid the bright light attacking her consciousness like a beam of fire searing through her retinas.

"She's back," Scabs said. He clicked the button on the back of the LED flashlight. "Thought maybe we'd lost you."

The room had been cleared out, though the posters of emo bands and skeletons adorned the walls remained. Erin sat in a plush chair that had come from downstairs. Her body had gone through the entire permutation, at least as fast as Scabs had seen with the others, he'd started milking in five random houses around east San Diego County. Sitting in the chair, she looked like something lost between human and animal. Her skin expanded at such a rate, and her musculature transformed so quickly, she was left with a roadmap of stretch lines and busted veins looking like destinations on the map of her bloated and contorted body. Her stomach grew as if impregnated. Her legs had gone thin and knobby at the knees and ankles. Toe and fingernails grew thick and long in a matter of hours. Being immobile in the chair, her appendages were of little use to her anyhow. Scabs was still figuring out a way to dispose of his Hags' limbs. All he really needed were living torsos. He'd read a story years ago about a man who'd used living human torsos to incubate babies that he sold on the black market.

Both of her arms were restrained to the chair, palm up. From the crooks of her elbows IV drips were inserted, connected to bags of liquid dope, a special blend Scabs whipped up for the queen hags. So potent it would kill a man, but strong enough to incapacitate the queens, who, as a side effect of the transformation, had become superhuman in strength, primarily through some sort of hidden power of the mind that humans had not possessed previously. Scabs himself didn't understand it, but did his best to quell them so there weren't any disasters.

Moving around Erin, who sat docile on the chair, Scabs checked and rechecked his machinery. He checked IV connections, tube insertions, and made sure his machines were functioning. Checked his customized computer program.

"I think we're ready," he said to the two half creatures who were assisting. The ones who had gone full tweaker creature were of no use to him. They became sloppy and unpredictable, making rookie mistakes out of basic tasks. That was an oversight he hoped to rectify, but changing the very DNA of human beings was kind of a Wild West frontier sort of deal.

The back of the chair in which Erin sat was cut out to allow access to her spinal column, from which sprouted a tube that had been carefully inserted there by Scabs.

"Here we go," Scabs said.

He typed in a command which started the process of extraction. The three looked upon Erin as she sat there, her eyes staring back at them, half closed from the sedation, the cocktail of drugs being fed through her veins. Scabs eyed the tube protruding from her spinal column with great interest. The tube remained empty for a time, and though he had done this with others, there was a niggling feeling it wasn't going to work, but sure enough, spinal fluid slowly inched its way through the tube.

Scabs had been itching his arms and neck so much in anticipation his fingertips were bloody. He wiped the blood on his lab coat, never taking his eyes off the slow drain of spinal fluid. He watched as it traveled down the plastic tubing and finally into a test tube, one drip at a time. It was a slow process, but the extraction was liquid gold.

Satisfied, he let out a sigh of relief. "It works."

The men who were assisting him didn't say much. They were grunt workers high as hell on speed and would do anything for the man who kept them that way. Just pawns, really.

"Keep an eye on her," Scabs said. "Switch out

the test tube when it's about a quarter inch from filled. Use the plastic stoppers to seal it and place it in the rack in the fridge. It's best kept chilled. I have the air set to sixty-three degrees. Keep it that way. Do you understand?"

They nodded.

"I'll be back shortly with the bedpan modification. She shouldn't have to release her bowels or urinate any time soon. Her diet is strictly narcotic at this point. With a supplement of vitamins and nutrients."

One of the men cringed at the thought of a bedpan modification.

"If there are any issues at all, get me immediately. I'll be getting everything else set up."

As he was leaving the room, a voice within his mind taunted him: *Leaving so soon?*

Scabs paused, closed his eyes, and took a deep breath. Yeah, she was a strong one. He started off again. By the time he got to the stairwell, one of his guys hollered, "The bitch is shitting herself! Fuck, it smells awful!"

Erin's bubbling laughter erupted in Scabs' mind.

CHAPTER 23

—--—

Amber barely made it out of the house on Second Street with her life. She clobbered Leche with the glass bong, surprised when it hit hard but didn't break. Then something inside came out in a tidal crash. She thwacked him repeatedly. The glass held up to the abuse as the rounded bottom of the water pipe smashed his face and head into a lumpy mess of flesh. It was as if his skull lacked bone density, the way it crumbled within the soft, mushy flesh.

Strangely, the tweaker creature who seemed so menacing just sat there on the couch and watched, as if braining people was a spectator sport. With the front door open, Amber looked back just to make sure Leche was out cold. He was dead, had to be.

The tweaker creature had already reached over the table and procured the little box. Amber cringed. The lanky beast would probably cram a couple rocks up its ass and drop dead of an overdose in no time. Just seeing the alien thing caused a tremble to run through her body, sending shivers up her spine.

With her adrenalin racing, Amber jumped into her car and turned the ignition. She put it in reverse to back onto Second Street and get the fuck out of there, but hesitated. It had been a long time since she'd been this fucked up. Her mind was sharp, like everything was in hyper focus. It was an 8K high-def reality and it frightened her. Everything sounded crisp and transmitted straight into her ears. Every movement was jerky, which was more startling because she recognized this, unlike the average speed freak. Her body heat was rising, sweat breaking out. Paranoia catapulted her into yet another echelon of madness.

Her eyes felt as if they were bulging from her face. She realized how quick and rapid her breathing became, and thought she was about to have a heart attack. Just then the door to the house opened. Several of the lanky human distortions emerged, sickly mushroom people. They were blindingly pale with heavy blue veins wrapping up their bodies like leafless vines. Three of them came out, faces alien. No noses or ears anymore. A cranium that was almost light bulb shaped. Eyes leaden with blood and all but dangling by the optic nerves. The mouths hung slack and toothless. One of them had gone next-level and didn't even have a jaw.

At first, they moved slowly, but then they saw Amber and went into a frenzied run. Amber tensed. A strange cramping pain jolted down her spine. She put the car in reverse again, this time backing up without a care in the world to her state of toxicity. She wasn't happy about having to drive high on super meth, but she wasn't about to allow those things to drag her back into the house. There was no telling what they'd do to her.

One thing Amber remembered from her visits to this house back in the day was the traffic on Second Street made backing out a chore. Right now, with a gaggle of rancid meth fueled monsters after her, it was much more treacherous. She backed to the edge of the driveway and looked over her should both left and right. She'd go whichever way she could, but there was traffic coming from both sides, as always.

Something impacted her car, jolting her hyper-attention forward. One of the creatures lunged onto the hood. Just then another slammed its body up against the door.

Amber yelped, not even thinking about the traffic on the road. The car shot backwards. The creature pressing against the door was unable to hold on and fell. The front tire rolled over its legs, crushing them. The one on the hood held tight, but as soon as Amber cranked the wheel left, putting the car into position to head down the road, it rolled off to the side, an unsightly lump of bone and flesh hardly resembling a human in its twisted state on the asphalt.

Amber hit the gas pedal and took off, squealing down the road. The car behind her had to hit its breaks, but couldn't avoid slamming into the curled up thing in the road. Like most cars coming around the bend on Second Street, it was going too fast. The impact batted the body, arms and legs akimbo, and that's the last Amber saw of the Second Street house.

Amber drove without a destination. She turned onto Broadway. She'd been down that road so many times in her life. It was super familiar, and so was the feeling of being high, though she had never done dope so powerful after only one small line. The further she drove, the more she felt a deep urge to do more. It was a nasty, incessant feeling, kind of like eating nothing all day and dealing with violent hunger pains.

Fuck, bitch, you don't need that shit. You did what you did to get out of that house. You're safe now. Forget the dope.

But she couldn't, and that frightened her. After just one line, she was craving like a son of a bitch.

She drove on, wondering if she should stop

somewhere. Was it safe to be driving like this? Certainly not, but she was very aware of her surroundings, and she was being cautious.

What was she going to do with herself? She hadn't found Erin, she had no idea where these other dope houses were, sprinkled around El Cajon, and she had a brain full of speed. Really, really good speed.

What the fuck! What the fuck!

Approaching Mollison Avenue, Amber made the quick decision to go to Mother's house. That was the last place she wanted to show up high on meth, but she would just have to explain herself. Mother would understand. At least then Amber would have a place to sober up.

Mother would make her soup. Mother would take care of her. Once the meth wore off and the urges subsided, they could put their heads together and continue the search for Erin.

But when Amber got to her mother's house, something wasn't right... or was the meth making her paranoid?

CHAPTER 24

—-—

Jason Weiler was supposed to sit watch over Erin, but he'd been terrified since getting to the new hag house. It wasn't Erin that frightened him, but all of the shadow people. He'd started seeing shadow people weeks ago, had even become used to them. They didn't say anything, but sometimes they would gesture to him. He never followed their lead, figuring they were trying to get him to do something that would get him killed. Even as carefree as he felt on the super meth, he didn't trust the them. His uncle Chester had been a massive speed freak back when Jason was growing up. Uncle Chester would always talk about the shadow people. If there was one thing he told Jason, it was to never listen to them. *Don't listen to 'em. Don't trust 'em.*

To this day, Jason loathed them, and he was terrified to see so many of them in the house. He'd seen his share, but never in these kinds of numbers.

Scabs found Jason at the bottom of the stairs and asked him, "Have you checked on her recently?"

Jason hesitated, feeling ashamed. "I can't get by all the shadow people."

Scabs reared back. "The what?"

Jason swallowed hard, then ran his tongue across his toothless maw. "Shadow people. There's a bunch of them up there." Jason's eyes shifted violently toward the landing at the top of the stairs, never really settling on anything, as if the very sight of the shadow people would do him harm.

Scabs looked up at the landing. "There's no one up there. You're just paranoid."

Jason looked up, then away, his face twisted in a hellish grimace. "You don't see them?" He sounded like a kid who was afraid of the boogey man in his closet.

"There's no one up there but Erin, and she needs to be monitored. The vial collecting her nectar probably needs to be changed. Get the fuck up there and do it!"

"But... but I can't get by them. There are just too many of them. They—"

Scabs pulled a scalpel out of the large pocket of his lab coat and dragged it across Jason's neck. He pushed hard. The blade was sharp and had no trouble severing his throat and carotid artery. Jason dropped to the floor, grasping his neck, and bled out onto the carpet. Scabs took the stairs and checked on Erin himself.

The vial didn't need to be changed yet, but was close. Everything seemed to be going smoothly. Erin appeared calm. The monitor showed her vitals were in average territory.

After a moment of hesitation, Scabs asked, "Are you doing something to mess with their minds?"

Erin spoke in his mind. "No. The shadow people come. I don't call for them, they gravitate to me."

"Can you," Scabs felt a chill if uncertainty run up his spine, "make them go away?"

"Who says I want to?"

Erin's eyes rolled back into her head. Scabs studied her as she lay there. He scratched at his arms, liberating a dusting of scabs. He figured she was drifting off the way she did, but entirely wasn't sure. She was probably just listening to his thoughts.

***

Erin drifted in a state between realms. She called to the shadow people, bringing them forth, into her consciousness. She'd tucked them away, ignoring so she didn't have to see them all around. They had multiplied since before. There were so many of them it was like a giant cloak of black filling the room in an all-consuming darkness.

Erin drifted back to the real world. She spoke in Scabs' mind. *You don't see them, the shadow people?*

"No. I don't see anything."

So, you're not using your product then, are you?

Scabs stood there for a moment longer and then left the room.

***

After leaving Erin's room Scabs asked everyone in the house if they could see the shadow people. They all nodded. "Yeah," Marco said, "this place is stupid with them. Especially upstairs."

"Why hasn't anyone told me about these shadow people?" he said, but Marco just stared at him like an idiot.

The only person who hadn't seen the shadow people was Larry.

Scabs accosted Larry. "So, you really aren't taking the super meth, are you?"

Larry hesitated before saying anything. "No, man. I see what it does to people. I'm not stupid."

Scabs narrowed his eyes and reached into his lab coat.

"Gonna slit my throat like you did Jason? Sorry, I'm not as stupid as everyone else." Larry smirked.

"Something tells me you don't use the shit either. You and me, we're smart." Larry shook his head. "I don't want to see any shadow people."

Now Scabs hesitated. "What I do or don't do is none of your business." Scabs stared deep into Larry's eyes for a moment. He hadn't seen eyes so lucid in quite some time. "Get out of here."

Larry tilted his head, his eyes darting to the hand Scabs had in his lab coat.

"Go now, before I change my mind."

Larry turned and left the house.

The remaining tweakers, all of them in various states of change, sat on the couch and love seat in the living room watching TV. They glanced upstairs from time to time, shuddering when they did so, which Scabs thought was odd because one of his observations about the change was that the tweaker creatures lost all functions of morality, along with most of their decision making skills, which caused them to lack emotional response and empathy. For whatever reason, the shadow people scared the shit out of them.

"I want one of you up there to check on her. Ignore the fucking shadow people. Go up two at a time, I don't care. Just be sure to go up there and change the vial. Got it?"

They all nodded, but Scabs figured they would all pull a Jason and chicken out.

Got to do something about those fucking shadow people, he thought.

Scabs went into the office and closed the door behind him. He sat down in the chair behind a mahogany desk, pondering how he would proceed. His thoughts went back to Erin, over and over. She was on an awfully large dosage of sedatives, and yet she seemed as strong as ever. More sedation? Even thinking that caused him to feel uncomfortable. She could be listening.

What's she gonna do, he thought, squash my brain like she did Jerry?

Maybe. Erin laughed and laughed.

Scabs collapsed over the desk wondering for the first time whether this was all worth it.

CHAPTER 25

—·—

Amber pulled up to her mother's house and parked along the curb. She found it strange there were so many cars parked in front of the house. Not in the driveway, but on the curb out front, which was unusual. Visitors would park on the curb in front of a house, but rarely were there so many random cars. Old junkers that were just about ready to give up the ghost.

She sat there collecting her thoughts. The meth was ridiculously strong, and it was sticking with her. The last thing Amber wanted was to go inside and have her mother know she was on drugs. She'd have to explain, of course, but she wanted to do the explaining on her terms. Even then, Mother might not believe and think she was using again, that drugs were the real reason she went AWOL. That's what Amber feared worse, her mother wouldn't believe her.

You must go in there. Just tell her the truth and she'll believe. Then you both can look for Erin. If you make that effort, she'll know your heart is true. Just don't tell her about the motel. No one needs to know about that.

Thinking about the incident at the motel gave Amber the strength to get out of the car and face her fears of possible rejection. After what she'd done there, not to mention what she'd done only an hour ago at the Second Street drug den, there was nothing to fear. The only objective was to find Erin.

The evening air was cool and welcoming on

Amber's skin. She hadn't realized how stuffy the car had been. As she walked up the driveway, something seemed off kilter. She chalked it up to the fact that she was still high as a kite, but something nagged at her subconscious.

At the door she hesitated, deciding how she would proceed. Well, she'd never knocked on her mother's door before. This had always been her house, the place she'd grown up. She couldn't think of one time she knocked to get in, therefore Amber reached into her purse, grabbing her keys. She unlocked the door and walked in.

The TV was on. Amber decided to holler for her mother rather than put the fear of God into the woman by suddenly walking into the living room. "Mom! It's Amber. I'm home!"

She walked down the hallway into the living room, and that's when she saw three tweaker creatures on her mother's couch smoking dope from a glass pipe. Amber stopped dead in her tracks, so startled that she dropped her purse on the ground.

"What the fuck are you doing in here?"

The three looked over at her, their bloody eyes like warning signs, but they didn't make a move, just sucked on the pipe and blew out smoke.

"Get the fuck out of here! What the hell are you doing in here? And where's my mother?"

One of the monstrous things stood. It was lanky and tall, face hideously distorted. It wore sweat shorts and a t-shirt, but the fabric was all splotchy with blood and weird stains.

"Stay the fuck back!" Amber yelled. "Where's my mother? Where the fuck is she?"

Then the other two creatures stood. The first one lunged after Amber, and though she was fast, the thing doubled her leg span and caught her easy enough, wrapping his knobby arms around her and digging his nails into the flesh around her breasts. He pulled her close, breathing his toxic breath down her neck.

"This is a hag house," the thing hissed, sloppily speaking through a mouth devoid of teeth. "What are *you* doing here?"

***

Suddenly, Erin was hit with a new sense of nostalgia. It attacked her much like walking into the house. Her mother's house. She squirmed and shifted in the chair, but her body was all but useless.

Deep down in the darkest pits of her new consciousness, the real Erin awakened by the sense of nostalgia. Having been pushed so far away from reality, Erin's old consciousness completely sobered. With the heavy vibes of nostalgia, images flashed in her old consciousness like slides. Pictures filed away and all but forgotten. Her sister Amber on Christmas morning, laughing. Playing outside. Riding her bike. Dressed up for Halloween. Eating a hotdog on a summer day and getting mustard on her shirt. Crying from a spill off her bike. So many memories Erin hadn't thought of for years. They came flooding, and her old consciousness rose to the surface of the damaged mind now inhabiting her mutated body.

Erin banished her new consciousness, pushing it even further away. She hoped it would stay there, festering in all of her bad memories. The new consciousness was strong. It would fight back.

There wasn't much time.

Erin used the power her mutated body possessed and traveled through the ethers of the house, seeking out the source of the psychic nostalgic energy. It wasn't hard to find. Downstairs, a woman was being mistreated by one of the gruesome looking tweaker creatures. Erin sensed a great love for the woman. The nostalgic energy radiated from her. And then, when the creature threw the woman onto the ground, Erin got a good look at her face. She recognized her sister.

A current of emotion swarmed in on Erin, much like the shadow people had done, only this was pure emotion, swelling within the hull of her monstrous being. She became enraged, having seen her sister thrown to the floor like a piece of garbage.

In that moment, the mutated half of her consciousness tried to find a weak spot and take over her mind, but Erin's old consciousness was sober and quick to push aside, she just didn't know how long she could fight before the new consciousness won, for she knew the power it possessed.

Erin focused on the shadow people, allowing herself to see them once again, and there were even more than ever. Though Erin had been banished deep into her subconscious, she'd been doing her best to watch and learn. At first the shadow people frightened her, but once she realized they could be banished, she'd felt more at ease. Now that she had control, she understood they were there to serve her.

Destroy the creatures attacking my sister! she demanded.

The shadow people poured down the stairs as if fighting for the honor of their beloved hag.

***

The throw to the ground was brutal, jarring

Amber almost to the point of unconsciousness. She'd heard about seeing stars after a massive knock to the head, and now she could honestly say she'd seen them.

A creature hovered over her, the one who grabbed and threw her to the ground. It was not as far gone as the one she saw at the Second Street house. This one still had his junk intact, which was made clear to Amber when he dropped his shorts. The thing between his legs was worse for wear, as if he'd spent time fucking a cheese grater. She cringed, disgusted with the rotting sausage.

He grabbed and stroked it, trying to get it hard, but it just wasn't happening. Amber tried to retreat by scooting backwards, but she ran into one of the other ones. He whispered in her ear, "Don't worry. Mine fell off days ago."

Some unseen force grabbed the tweaker with the rancid cock and throw him onto the ground. In that instant the others made frightened sounds and tried to get away, but both of them were pinned down, flailing and gyrating but unable to move.

Watching them, Amber saw the faint shapes of some ghostly black forms, like people made of shadow. They flickered in her vision, holding down the three tweaker creatures. They were merely black shapes in human form, but their shadowy hands were sharp at the ends of the fingertips. They used these claws to eviscerate the tweakers, disemboweling them, ripping their flesh off like a bear scratching the trunk of a tree. They were relentless. Blood was shed, flying and splattering on the walls. Amber tried to get away, but couldn't remove herself fast enough to be spared from a spattering of hot tweaker blood.

From the kitchen she watched. Now the shadow people were once again invisible to her, which made the mayhem much more absurd. Slashes appeared out of nowhere. Blood flew from the bodies. Limbs were extracted. Faces skinned to the skull. Guts hurled into the air, and flung this way and that, decorating the stair railing and the walls in a macabre display like art.

The office door beside the kitchen opened and a man emerged dressed in slacks and a white lab coat, dotted with dried blood. Amber clenched up at the sight of him, and then recoiled when she realized his flesh was covered in a skin of scabs.

"What the hell is going on out here?" Dr. Scabs said.

CHAPTER 26

Noticing Amber, Dr. Scabs said, "Who are you and what are you doing here?" Before she can respond, Erin says, *she's my sister.*

Suddenly, the garage door busted open and a couple of tweakers who weren't in quite as bad shape as the others burst through. Though no one in the room could see them, the shadow people converged on the duo and ripped them to shreds, much like they did to the other three, making quick work of them as they screamed.

"What the fuck is going on," Scabs said as he watched two men get spontaneously torn to pieces.

"It's shadow people," Amber said.

Scabs tilted his head questioningly. "You don't look like the type—"

Leave her alone!

***

It was hard for Erin to remain in Scabs' mind for too long. He was sick. His brain operated on a bizarre level of psychosis that made her feel as if she were going insane, but she had to get in there, for the sake of her sister. If only she could get a grip on his mind to immobilize him.

Erin drifted into Scabs' consciousness, fighting for purchase among the madcap thoughts swirling like a hurricane. It was a struggle, but she did her best to avoid being swept up in his madness. The fight for the psychosis of Scabs was so demanding that her new consciousness found a weak spot, emerging from the depths.

The aura of the new consciousness was like a dark infection. Erin fought to banish it, but as she did, Scabs' madness seeped in, causing her to lose control.

Go away, Erin said.

You're mine now, bitch! I should have the shadow people destroy what's left of your soul.

I don't need you! Just go back where you came from.

Never! This isn't even your body anymore. You do not exist anymore.

Fuck off! Erin corralled her inner strength and mentally shoved her new consciousness.

***

Dr. Scabs grabbed his head and closed his eyes tight. He gritted teeth, spittle squirting through the gaps as he breathed in heavy intervals.

"Get them out of my head," he said.

Amber retreated further into the kitchen. With five bodies completely flayed down to red bones and torn muscle, and now a man of scabs who was clearly losing his mind, she was in serious danger, not to mention she still didn't know where her mother was.

Scabs moaned and screamed, clutching his head, and swinging it around like he could fling the voices from his mind.

Amber scanned the kitchen for something she could use to defend herself, all the time keeping an eye on Scabs, who seemed to be on the verge of complete mental collapse. She frantically looked through the drawers, but there was nothing.

You've got to listen to me.

The voice came out of nowhere, startling Amber. She looked around the room, as if someone might have snuck in there and whispered into her ear, but no one was there. Scabs slopped in the blood and human meat-soaked carpet, fighting with his own mind.

It's me. It's Erin. You have to kill him. I can only hold him for so long, and I'm losing control. Please, you must kill him. He's the one who's responsible for all of this. He has the lives of hundreds on his soul. Mine as well. Kill him. NOW!

She didn't know how Erin was speaking in her head like that, but she knew without a doubt it was her voice. Tears welled in Amber's eyes, blurring her vision.

"The voices!" Scabs yelled. "Get the fuck out of my head, you bitch!"

An image flashed in Amber's mind, one of her mother baking cookies at Christmas time. In her hands was a big ol' wooded rolling pin. Amber couldn't say for sure that the image had come from her own subconscious, for she couldn't really remember, but she knew where the rolling pin was. Sure enough, tucked away behind the pots and pans at the very back of the cabinet she found it. Pulling it out, she hefted the thing, judging its weight. Seemed like it would do the job.

I can't hold him much longer. Erin's voice exploded in Amber's mind, exasperated and weak.

With no time for hesitation or moral quibble, Amber rushed the scabbed man and bashed his head with the rolling pin, taking him by complete surprise. He went down hard, but wasn't out. Amber bashed him again, but he squirmed even more.

"What the fuck?" Scabs said as he twisted and contorted on the ground.

Amber dashed into the kitchen, dropped the rolling pin and remembered the drawer where her mother kept the knives. She grabbed the biggest one she could find.

Amber doubled back to Scabs and drew the knife across his throat. Quick and easy. Or so she thought.

He rolled onto his side and was grasping at his neck, blood gushing through his fingers. He gurgled out words, but they were muffled by the blood erupting from his mouth. He gurgled and choked; it was the worst damn thing Amber had heard in her life. She clamped her hands over her ears, just hoping the poor fuck would die already, but he had a little bit left in the tank. He crawled across the floor, his neck leaking like a busted gutter in a rainstorm. Crawling toward Amber. His scabbed face was all torn and bloody, repulsive. Amber backed away, and then something got into her, almost as if someone was using her body like a marionette, she lunged forward, knife poised, and stabbed Scabs right in the left eye. She then twisted the knife, digging into his brain, creating a massive, cavity where his eye had been. This final blow took the last vestiges of life from the madman the tweakers called Dr. Scabs.

Amber let go of the knife and took several steps back. The scene was awful, the torn eye leaked down scabbed flesh, the red gooey brain matter seeping from the eye socket. She bent over and vomited on the floor.

Crumpled into a ball, Amber wept.

She took all the time she needed. No one entered the house. No tweakers. No creatures. No scabbed men. She just wept until she could compose herself, and then she went in search of her mother.

She's gone, a voice said in Amber's mind, but not quite the voice of her sister.

"Mom! Mom!" Amber hollered as she ascended the stairs.

No response came.

She's gone.

Amber made a growling sound. "Get the fuck out of my head!"

She checked the rooms, starting with her mother's. Nothing there. It hadn't even been disturbed. She checked the closet and the bathroom, but those too were clean and tidy, as always. Amber went to the next bedroom, which had been her room before she left. Would have been her room after the academy too, until she found herself an apartment. She opened the door and was hit with the familiar smell of her perfume mixed with the stringent, coppery odor of blood. On the floor in a pile like yesterday's garbage was a body. She recognized the nightgown, one her mother wore often. Amber knelt beside the body and looked at the face.

And she broke down.

CHAPTER 27

I don't have much time. I don't know how long I can keep the creature away.

The voice in Amber's mind was again her sisters. As terrifying as it was to have a voice suddenly speak to her like that, she was somewhat comforted it was Erin.

Amber bolted from her room and down the hall. She burst into Erin's room to find something of a horror show. The creature was almost twice the size of a normal human, sitting in a chair that Amber recognized, taken from downstairs. The thing's head was overly large and oblong, as if it the skull grew and expanded. The arms and legs were thin, like twiggy branches with knobby elbows and knees. Her belly protruded as if pregnant, covered in tiny welts and boils, some of which had burst, leaking a sticky substance not unlike gooey pus.

The creature swiveled its head, almost painfully, and then opened its eyes. They were human eyes. Amber's mouth dropped. She recognized them as Erin's eyes. They were pale blue and gorgeous in the hideous face of a monster. Amber had always been jealous of her sister's eyes.

The creature's mouth moved. It tried to speak, choking on the words for it hadn't used its voice in some time. After several attempts, it found its voice and croaked out a sentence. "It's me. I just don't look or sound like me. He changed me." The creature sighed. "There's no hope for me. I cannot live in this disgusting body. I can't even move anymore. There are others like me. We produce the substance that makes the meth... super." The creature coughed, and then seemed to struggle. "It's hard to hold the new me back, but I swear I'll do away with all of us. All the hags. We're not queens. We never were."

Amber didn't quite know what to make of this. She stood there staring at something very similar to the tweaker creatures she'd been exposed to over the past forty-eight hours, but was it really her sister? The pale blue eyes said it was.

"Please go," the creature said, "before the new consciousness takes over. I have one last thing to do. Then it will all be done."

Amber didn't know what to say. This thing wasn't her sister. It couldn't be.

But those eyes.

I love you, Erin said in Amber's mind, in the soft voice she very much recognized.

"I love you too."

Amber walked out of the room and closed the door.

***

After Amber left, Erin summoned the shadow people. The crowded around, almost completely blacking her out.

"Go. Find the others like me. The hags. One by one. Smother them. Drown them in your shadow. But first you must crowd around, smother me. Take me away. Take me into your darkness."

The shadow people crowded around Erin, pushing their way into the room and piling on top of one another until the entirety of the room was filled with darkness.

***

Amber went downstairs, aimlessly walking through a house of hellish horrors. She found refuge in the office where Scabs had been using her mother's computer. He'd also been busy making notes on loose papers. Amber idly looked at the papers, but her mind was elsewhere. She was drawn to the office since it hadn't been turned into a bloodbath.

Now what?

She stood there looking at the papers Scabs had written on. One of them appeared to be some sort of suicide note. Amber picked it up for closer inspection. He wrote about creating the super meth, about testing on his wife before she died, about how he regretted everything. It was strange, reading the words of a man she'd killed who was apparently going to do himself in anyway. At the end of the letter, he wrote about the voices in his head. That Erin wouldn't stop. That she was going to kill him if she continued. She was too strong.

She left the room and went back upstairs. Erin's door was open. Amber stood back and listened, but heard nothing. She then turned the corner and saw nothing but blackness within the room. A deep, swelling black formed of many things human in shape, twisting and turning, molting together.

The shadow people.

Amber stepped closer to the black mass. She saw herself walking into it, becoming absorbed in the darkness. Swallowed up and never heard from again. At peace with her mother and sister.

But she couldn't do it.

Then the opportunity was over. The shadow people fled the room one by one, passing by Amber as they left, some even passing through her. As they drifted by, they faded away, hopefully the last vestiges of the meth she'd taken earlier. Once they were all gone and the room came back into view, the chair in which the creature had been sitting was empty. The medical equipment now dangling unused, the monitor beeping.

Erin left her mother's house, and the world outside seemed just a little bit darker.

ABOUT THE AUTHOR

Robert Essig is the author of over a dozen books including *Stronger Than Hate, Death Obsessed,* and *Shallow Graves* (with Jack Bantry).

He has published well over 100 short stories, most recently in *Double Barrel Vol. 3* and *Welcome to the Splatter Club.*

He is the editor of the anthology *Chew on This!* Robert lives with his family in East Tennessee.

Find out what he's been up to at robertessig.blogspot.com

NOVELS AVAILABLE FROM
THE EVIL COOKIE PUBLISHING

ANTHOLOGIES AVAILABLE
FROM
THE EVIL COOKIE PUBLISHING

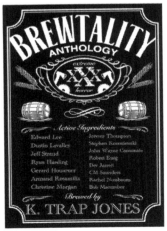

www.theevilcookie.com